"I should leave."

Then he saw the fire. Burning deep within her amazing black eyes and it was a heat like none he'd ever seen before. Desire had caught her in its spell just as it had him, and she was feeling the same undertow of attraction that he was feeling.

"Yes," he said, reaching out to touch her gently. "You should leave."

Her gaze moved to his lips and Travis felt the air whoosh from his lungs. Damn, she looked as hungry as he felt, and he found himself moving closer.

"I really, *really* should leave," she said, but her words were meaningless since she was still staring at his mouth.

"Yes. Leaving would be the smart thing to do."

"And I'm very smart," she answered. She met his gaze once more, and a teasing, tempting smile formed. "Or at least I used to be."

Dear Reader,

Ah, love. It's magical, isn't it? That first spark of attraction. The thrill of falling deeply in love. That wonderful tingly feeling you get. Nothing can compare.

Speaking of magic, my heroine, Dani Karlinski, has a problem. Her grandmother puts romantic curses on people, and now one of them is threatening to sue. Dani wants to help, so she enlists the aid of an old high school friend, Travis Walker, to disprove these supposed magical spells.

Unfortunately, Dani and Travis keep finding that her grandmother's curses *do* seem to come true. How can that be? Magic isn't real. But who can deny there's something enchanting about falling in love?

I hope you enjoy Dani and Travis's story. I also hope you find the magic of love yourself. It is, after all, what makes life fun.

All the best,

Liz Jarrett

P.S. Please stop by my Web site www.lizjarrett.com. There's always something new and fun happening.

Books by Liz Jarrett

HARLEQUIN TEMPTATION
827—TEMPTING TESS
984—EVERY STEP YOU TAKE...

HARLEQUIN DUETS
67—CATCHING CHASE
   NABBING NATHAN
87—MEANT FOR TRENT
   LEIGH'S FOR ME

LIZ JARRETT

A LITTLE NIGHT MAGIC

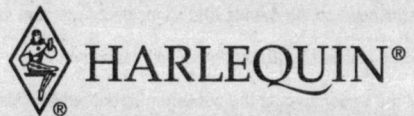

HARLEQUIN®

TORONTO • NEW YORK • LONDON
AMSTERDAM • PARIS • SYDNEY • HAMBURG
STOCKHOLM • ATHENS • TOKYO • MILAN • MADRID
PRAGUE • WARSAW • BUDAPEST • AUCKLAND

To my husband.
Thanks for making the past nineteen years magical!
and
To the wonderful folks at Harlequin Toronto, especially my editor,
Kathryn Lye. I appreciate everything you've done.

ISBN 0-373-69220-X

A LITTLE NIGHT MAGIC

Copyright © 2005 by Liz Lounsbury.

www.eHarlequin.com

Printed in U.S.A.

1

TRAVIS WALKER reread the message in his hand. Client wants help with grandma's curses. Meeting at 1:00. What was this? Had Walker Investigations really sunk to helping gutter-mouthed grandmas? If his brother wasn't away on his honeymoon, Travis would dismiss this as another of Max's jokes.

But the lucky devil was in the Bahamas experiencing the joys of wedded bliss. No, this note was the handiwork of their new office intern, Elvin Richards, aka The Favor. Travis had been dating Elvin's aunt at the time he'd agreed to hire the college kid. Hey, at certain times, a man would agree to just about anything.

Unfortunately, the sexy aunt with amazing legs was long gone, but Walker Investigations was still stuck with Elvin. That would teach him to make decisions with his heart and not his head.

And to be perfectly honest, he hadn't made that decision with his *heart*. Another part of his anatomy had been the main influencing factor.

Sure, he could fire the kid, but come on. How fair would that be? Plus, damn it, the kid was likeable.

How did you fire someone who was so genuinely cheerful? It would be like pink-slipping Santa Claus.

Even he wasn't that low.

"Elvin," he hollered, not wanting to mess with their new complicated phone system that had more buttons than a candy machine. Max loved it, but he hated it. "What does this message mean?"

Elvin popped his head into the doorway. A sandy-haired, all-American-looking kid, he was currently grinning that same grin he always grinned, regardless of the occasion. "What message, boss?"

"This one about the meeting." Travis waved the piece of paper. "What does it mean?"

Elvin bobbed his head and said slowly, "It means the lady wants us to help with her grandma's cursing."

Travis frowned. "I can read. What does it *mean*? Did you ask her for more information?"

Elvin kept grinning while he shook his head. "Nope. I took what you and Max said about offending potential clients to heart and didn't ask a thing." He glanced around, almost as if he thought someone would overhear him, then said softly, "I think her grandmother talks like a sailor. Mine used to. Could curse the sky blue, as my mom always said."

Travis didn't doubt for a moment that Elvin's grandmother had been on the unusual side. But that information didn't help his current situation.

"Next time, find out a little more," Travis said, mentally thanking fate that at least Max wasn't here to witness this. Max had made it clear that Elvin was Travis's problem, but, of course, like any brother, he took great joy in pointing out the major flaws in the hire-by-your-hormones approach to running a business.

"I'm really not good at finding out information. Besides, what more could I ask without prying?" Elvin blinked and looked sincerely baffled.

Blowing out a breath of frustration, Travis said slowly, "We're private investigators. Finding out information is our *business.*"

"Seems kind of rude."

Before Travis could answer—and a lot of possibilities were hovering on his tongue—the front doorbell rang softly, letting them know the client had arrived. Elvin scurried out of Travis's office and into the reception area. Travis stood and waited for Elvin to lead her in. When over a minute passed, he gave up and headed toward the lobby.

Elvin was sitting behind his desk, a dopey look on his face as he stared at the client. Yeah, real professional. Ogle the paying customers.

Travis glanced at the couch across the room and drew in a deep, purely male breath. Okay, so maybe Elvin had something of an excuse. The woman sitting on the couch was a tall, gorgeous brunette, the kind that came into private detectives' offices in the movies, but absolutely never showed up in real life.

The woman smiled at him, and Travis felt all the blood in his body rush southward. Then she slowly stood and headed toward him, a sexy smile on her lips, and an even sexier sway to her hips.

Oh, man.

"Hello," she said, her voice as seductive and sultry as the rest of her. As she drew closer, he couldn't help noticing how black her eyes were. Not brown. Black. A deep, night-sin black. The kind of eyes a man could drown in.

"Are you okay?" she asked, a slight frown forming on her face.

Travis mentally slapped himself. Great, he was standing there looking as idiotic as Elvin. Pulling himself together, he smiled and extended his hand. "Yes. Hi, I'm Travis Walker."

She took his hand in hers, but rather than shaking it, she tipped her head to the side and smiled slowly. "And I am?"

Ah, geez. Disappointment washed through him. A drop-dead gorgeous client finally walks into the place and it turns out she's a looney tune. Figured.

"Happy to see me?" he tried in a last-ditch hope that she wasn't insane.

Her expression didn't change, but the glimmer in her eyes dimmed. He literally could *feel* her disappointment. Travis scanned his brain. He must know her, but from where? The obvious answer was that he'd dated her at some point, but he knew that couldn't be true. He would remember a woman who looked like this.

Some things a man's DNA didn't let him forget.

"I'm Danielle. Danielle Karlinski," she said in that satin-sheet voice of hers. "Dani."

Recognition slammed into Travis like a runaway bulldozer. "Gypsy!"

She laughed, the sound as seductive as the rest of her. "I go by Dani now, Killer."

From across the room, Elvin asked, "Killer? Why did you call him Killer?"

It had been years since anyone had called Travis that. "It's a nickname from high school. Nothing special."

He'd intended to let it go at that, figuring Elvin didn't really need an explanation. But he'd forgotten that Gypsy was never at a loss for words.

After tossing a grin at Travis, Dani said to Elvin, "A group of us hung around together in high school. Everyone had a nickname. I was Gypsy because of my dark hair and eyes—"

Travis shook his head. "Nope. Not the reason. We called you Gypsy because your grandmother came to school and told us your family were gypsies."

"So not true," she said, laughing again. "And only someone as boneheaded as you guys were would have believed her." She looked at Elvin. "My father sells insurance and my grandfather ran a hardware store. Hardly gypsies."

Dani turned her attention back to him, and Travis couldn't help smiling. Damn, it was good to see her. She'd changed a lot during the years. In high school, she'd been skinny with big glasses.

Not anymore. Now she was beautiful. Tall, with generous curves and a sexy, slinky way of moving, she was a walking fantasy.

"Hello, Killer." Dani waved one hand in front of him. "Did you drift off on me?"

"I'm still here." Deciding there was no sense lying to her, especially since what he'd been thinking had probably been written all over his face, he confessed, "I was noticing how gorgeous you've become."

"Ah, that's so sweet, Killer. Thanks. I'd say you've changed, too, but well, you haven't." She laughed again. "Still quick with a line, I see."

"Hey," he protested. Sure, *sometimes* he used lines. Okay, maybe more often than just sometimes, but he wasn't using one now.

Still, one look at Dani's face told him she wasn't about to believe him.

"Oh, admit it, Trav," she said. "You're still a dog."

He started to protest again, then decided to try a different approach. He gave her his I've-been-bad look. That one never failed to turn women to mush. "I know I used to be wild in high school, but I'm an adult now. I meant what I said. You're beautiful, and not just on the outside. I can tell you're still as beautiful and sweet on the inside as you were when we were teens."

Dani met his gaze, her expression thoughtful. Travis barely resisted the temptation to do a victory dance. Yes! He'd known she'd be unable to resist the look. That one always won women over and made them believe—

"You're kidding, right?" Her laugh this time was more of a hoot. "You don't really say things like that to women, do you? You come across as very superficial." Dani patted his arm. "Travis, women know when men are lying to them. That line reeked of insincerity. As a trial lawyer, I've studied people, and I feel obligated to point out that when you lie to people, it's only because you have your own trust issues." She patted his arm again. "Maybe you should seek professional help."

Travis arched one eyebrow. "Cute. And hey, thanks for the concern, but I'll muddle through."

Dani gave him that look women gave to puppies. "Okay, but remember, there's no shame in admitting you have a problem."

He was aware that Elvin was hanging on everything they said, so he decided to move the conversation into his office.

"Your concern is overwhelming," he said dryly, but she only laughed again. He couldn't help smiling at the sound. Funny, he'd forgotten how much time they'd all spent laughing in high school. But now, seeing Gypsy, he had to admit, those had been great years.

"You didn't tell me why you call him Killer," Elvin pointed out, half leaning across the desk. "Did he do something bad in high school?"

Dani never took her gaze off Travis as she explained, "Travis was a real lady-killer. He had all the moves, and the girls were crazy about him."

"No, they weren't," Travis felt obligated to say. "It was just that as an army brat, I'd lived lots of places growing up, so I was more sophisticated than you hicks. You were easily impressed."

A slow smile formed on her face. It was a teasing smile, a tempting smile.

An amazingly sexy smile.

And once again, Travis felt attraction wrap around him and squeeze. She was one gorgeous lady.

"Travis? A lady-killer?" Elvin made a snorting, laughing, choking noise. "Travis?"

That brought him back to reality. Travis was all set to tell the kid that yeah, he'd been hot and heavy with the girls in high school when he realized that wouldn't help him convince Dani he was now a mature adult.

Instead, he said to Dani, "I know you must be busy. Come inside my office and tell me about your grandmother." He pushed open his door, and this time when he smiled at her, he used his all-business smile. As Dani walked by him, he didn't miss the smirk hovering around her lips. He also didn't miss the faint musky, sensuous smell of her perfume.

Once again, he felt his hormones take improper notice, so he looked at Elvin, knowing the kid would aggravate him and make him forget all about Dani.

His plan worked. One look at Elvin sitting at the receptionist's desk practically drooling made Travis grit his teeth.

"Don't you have some work to do?" he asked the younger man.

Elvin shrugged. "I guess. But this is more interesting." In a voice only slightly muted, he asked, "What do you think is up with her grandmother?"

"Let Travis come in here and I'll tell him," Dani hollered back.

Elvin looked stunned, obviously surprised Dani could hear him, but come on, people two offices away could hear him.

"Tell me later," Elvin said.

Travis frowned. "No. Now get back to work."

He headed inside his office, and as he shut the door, he noticed Elvin was hard at work playing a computer game.

"That kid," he muttered.

"Is probably looking at you as a father figure and only needs a male role model to teach him how to behave," Dani said.

"Is that your professional opinion as a student of human behavior?" he asked, coming to stand next to her.

"More or less. He's a smart young man who is trying to impress you."

At that moment, Elvin started singing the jingle from a local toy store's commercials. As he sang, he kept getting louder and more enthusiastic. Travis looked at Dani and raised an eyebrow. "I take it you're not very good at judging people."

"*Usually* I am," she said. "Maybe that young man needs a little more time to grow up."

"Yeah, a couple of hundred years should do it."

Again, she laughed. "Travis, it's so good to see you. I haven't laughed this much in years."

Then she did the one thing he'd been hoping she wouldn't since she'd woken up his libido.

She hugged him.

DANI WAS so glad she'd come to see Travis. Not only was she sure he would be able to help her, but she was truly happy to see him again. When she'd arrived at his office, she'd been stressed and worried, but now she felt calm. Calm was something she rarely felt these days, what with the pressure of the new job she was about to start in New York and the pressure from her family.

But Travis made her happy and reminded her of fun times, so she hugged him even tighter.

"Hello, old friend," she said.

Travis hugged her back. Having his arms around her made Dani feel safe and secure and...something else. Something she couldn't quite name. Something that felt like—

Desire.

With a start, Dani pulled away from Travis and stared at him. Okay, that was new. She'd never felt anything remotely like desire around Travis before. Never. Not even when all the girls in high school had been fawning over him, she'd always just thought of him as a platonic guy friend. She'd never wanted him, lusted after him or dreamt about him.

But that sure had changed a couple of seconds

ago. Now all she could think about was how handsome Travis was and how attracted she was to him.

Wow.

"Everything okay?" Travis asked.

Dani tried to determine from his expression if he knew what had just happened, but she couldn't tell a thing. Well, it didn't matter anyway because nothing like that was going to happen again. She had no intention of getting close enough to him for her emotions to go crazy again.

"I'm fine." She headed over to one of the chairs across the room and sat. After he was settled behind his desk, she said, "I'm in a little bit of a rush, so let me explain why I'm here."

"Sure. The message I got said it had to do with your grandmother cursing. So has her potty mouth gotten her into trouble or something?"

Dani rolled her eyes. "Potty mouth, please. My grandmother thinks *drat* is a hard-core cuss word."

"Then I'm confused."

That made two of them, because she was still more than a little rattled by what had happened when they'd hugged. She could still feel the tingle of attraction dancing across her skin and her breathing was none too steady. But years of difficult trials had taught her to stay focused, so she forced herself to stay on topic.

"I don't know how much you remember about my grandmother."

Travis leaned back in his chair. "She was…unique."

"Understatement of the year. When Nana Freda

gets upset at someone, she sometimes says something that she tells them is a prophecy, but that in actuality is just the rantings of an elderly woman."

Travis nodded, his expression serious. His demeanor was completely professional. "I see. So my only question is—huh?"

Despite herself, Dani felt a smile tug at her lips. She didn't want to find Travis amusing. Not now. Not after she'd just felt a jolt of lust shoot through her. She'd always been a sucker for a man with a great sense of humor.

"Is that why you need a detective? You need someone to track down the meaning of that sentence?" Again, he asked this with a straight face, and this time, Dani couldn't stop herself from smiling.

"Let me be clearer," she said.

"Sounds like a good plan."

"My grandmother goes around putting curses on people she thinks have wronged her. She's done this for years and years. My family thinks of it as her little idiosyncrasy."

"What sort of curses?" Travis asked. "Does she squint, point a gnarled finger, and mutter, 'You'll die a horrible death'?"

Dani sighed at his melodrama. She needed him to take this seriously. "They tend to be more romantic curses."

Travis scratched his jaw. "Romantic curses. Now there's a phrase you don't hear very often. Give me an example of a romantic curse."

Even after all these months, Dani still couldn't be-lieve how silly this sounded. "Here's the one that's causing all the problems. She told her dry cleaner that love would overwhelm him."

Travis gave her a pointed look. "And did it?"

She nodded. "Yes. He's a widower who got in-volved with a woman in her twenties and stopped paying attention to his business."

"Because? What? He was too busy bungling in the jungle?"

"Apparently," she said dryly. Then the reality of the situation forced her to admit, "And he feels this is my grandmother's fault."

Travis looked as if he was trying hard not to laugh. A kinder woman would have told him to go ahead and at least smile, but Dani decided it would be bet-ter for him if he learned early on how to handle this case without laughing. She needed him to take this seriously because the problems facing Nana Freda certainly were serious.

"Why love curses?" he asked.

"They're not love *curses*. My grandmother thinks that people in love are happy people. Happy people are nice. She likes nice people. So she helps them fall in love so they'll be nice."

"I see," he said, but Dani spotted the smile that was still lurking around his lips. "So why do you need a detective?"

She didn't miss the faint gust of laughter in his voice as he asked his question, but she chose to ignore it. "The dry cleaner says he's going to sue my grandmother. He claims she ruined his business and he thinks she should pay."

"And what do you want me to prove? That this guy was having sex but not more than he used to have before your grandmother cursed him?"

"No, because that won't help. Apparently he only lived for his business before he met this young woman. Then he let the business slide because, as he says, love overwhelmed him."

Travis scratched his chin. "No offense, but I don't think *love* was what he was experiencing."

"I agree, but I'm not sure a jury will see it our way." Dani looked him straight in the eyes and explained her carefully devised plan. "Instead, I want you to help me find other people my grandmother has cursed. If we can prove her curses had no effect on their lives, we stand a better chance of shooting down his argument."

Travis looked dubious. "But will that really help? You're a smart lawyer. Isn't it Psychology 101 that if you believe something is true, then it's true to you? Isn't that the theory behind curses and things like that? The person sincerely believes it to be true and therefore the curse works?"

"I've considered that, but still, finding other people who *didn't* believe in the curses can only help our case." She fiddled with the strap of her purse. Talking about this case always rattled her nerves. She hated anything bad happening to Nana Freda, but she also didn't have time for this right now. She'd finally landed a great job at a firm in New York and was due to start in a little under two weeks. She should be concentrating on clearing out her apartment here in Chicago and not on this case.

But her grandmother needed her, so how could she say no?

Travis was making some notes, so Dani said, "Trav, I need help on this. I know it may be a long shot, but it's the only idea I have. Everyone wants Nana to hand over all her savings, but I don't think she should have to do that. I think this man is using this as an excuse for his own foolishness."

Travis looked up and winked at her. "I think your plan just may work, Gypsy."

"Under the circumstances, I think you should avoid calling me Gypsy."

He smiled. "True. So do you have a list of people your grandmother has cursed?"

"Nana Freda wants to talk to you herself about them," Dani said. "She refused to give me the names. Instead, she wants me to bring you by the house so she can talk to you."

"When?"

"Whenever you can make it." She realized this was asking a lot. She hadn't seen Travis in years, and now she was expecting him to drop everything and help her.

"Now works for me," he said.

Dani hadn't expected him to be willing to go immediately, but it certainly made her life easier. She'd known instinctively that he wouldn't let her down. And she'd been right. "Great."

"Want to ride together or take separate cars?"

She didn't hesitate. "Separate cars."

"Makes sense." He made a few more notes, then asked, "Did Elvin tell you about our fees? I realize we're old friends—"

"It's no problem," she assured him. "And I insist on paying you the standard rate."

"Okay. Then why don't you give me directions to where we're going. I'll let Elvin know what's happening, and we can head out."

He stood and walked to the reception area. Dani readjusted her purse strap, then headed toward the door. For the first time in several weeks, she felt optimistic about this case. She had a good feeling that Travis really would be able to help her. And it was wonderful to see him again.

As she watched him talk to the young man behind the receptionist's desk, she couldn't help thinking how well he'd turned out. Her grandmother had asked her this morning if she thought Travis would still be a nice-looking young man. Dani had speculated that he'd be fat and bald.

But he was neither. He was still very nice-looking, if you could call a man who seemed to drip with raw sensuality "nice-looking." He was tall, still had all of his thick, dark chocolate-brown hair, *and* had that great smile.

But Travis's looks came from so much more than his features. His attitude and the way he carried himself, along with that twinkle of devilment that lurked in his eyes, all added up to an incredibly attractive man.

Personally, she'd never thought of him as sexy in high school. But she certainly did now. And for her own self-preservation, the sooner she got him working on this case and put some distance between them, the happier she'd be. Just like she didn't have time right now for this lawsuit, she certainly didn't have time to get distracted by a man.

So she'd keep her mind on the case—no matter how yummy Travis Walker had become.

2

Travis studied the front of Dani's parents' house and whistled softly. Man, her father was one heck of an insurance salesman. The place was huge. A rambling modern house painted bright white, it didn't seem like something a girl nicknamed Gypsy would grow up in.

He pulled around the wide circular drive in front and parked a little way beyond the front door. Climbing out of his car, he grinned at Dani. "If I'd known you were rich, I would have chased you in high school."

"No, you wouldn't," she said, shutting the door to her blue BMW. "You didn't date smart girls in high school. And as I'm sure you remember, I'm very smart."

He chuckled and headed across the wide driveway to join Dani. This case was going to be a lot of fun. Over the years, he'd thought a few times about the kids he'd hung around with in high school.

Up until he was a teenager, he'd moved from school to school almost every year because his father had been in the army. He'd never really got to make many school friends. But after they'd settled in Chicago, they'd stayed put for a few years. That's why once he and his brother got out of the navy, they'd moved back. They liked this town. It felt more like home than any other place they'd ever lived in. In fact, he still kept in touch with a couple of the guys from the old high-school gang.

Almost as if she'd read his mind, Dani asked, "Do you still see Will or Mike or Brian?"

Interesting how she'd only mentioned the males. "I see Brian every few weeks. We get together at the gym and play a game or two of basketball. He's an engineer now."

"I can't picture Brian playing basketball," she said, leading the way up the front steps. "He was always a two-left-feet kind of guy."

"He's outgrown it." Then with a smile, he added, "Now he's got two right feet."

Dani laughed. "No wonder you like to play against him."

"Got to get your small victories where you can find them in this world," he said. He liked her smile. Liked it a lot. He liked her eyes, too.

His gaze drifted to her lips. They were full and looked soft. She wasn't wearing any sort of gloss, but her lips were still a dark pink and suddenly, all Travis could think of was how much he'd like to kiss those soft, full lips. Slow, lingering kisses that would let him explore her—

"Stop it."

Travis pulled his gaze up to meet hers. "Stop what?"

"That look you were giving me. Don't do it."

"What look?" he teased, knowing darn well what she was talking about.

"That, oh-baby-I-could-eat-you-up look."

Travis laughed. "I would never, *ever* say something like that."

"Yeah, well your look does," she muttered, then rang the doorbell. "So don't do it again. Just because I'm female doesn't mean you have to hit on me."

"I wasn't hitting on you. Did you hear one single 'Oh, baby' leave my lips?"

She gave him an oh-pulease look, and he chuckled.

"Okay, sorry. But a guy doesn't get called a lady-killer if he's not interested in women. It's a habit of mine."

"One you need to break."

He could tell she wanted to say more, but the door flew open and a blur of bright blue rushed out and wrapped itself around Dani like a blanket.

"Danielle, you tell your mother that I'm not signing any papers. I didn't do a thing wrong, so I refuse to give him my money."

Travis tried to look around Dani to see who was speaking, but all he caught was a glimpse of white hair.

"Nana Freda, leave Mom to me. I'll explain our plan."

"Good."

The blue blanket pulled itself off Dani, and then took a flying leap toward him.

"Whoa," Travis said, stopping it just before he was engulfed. "Hold on there."

A tiny woman wearing a bright-blue dress and wrapped in an equally bright-blue shawl blinked up at him. She had long silver earrings dangling from her earlobes, several chunky silver necklaces draped around her neck, and climbing up each arm were what Travis conservatively estimated to be twenty-five silver bracelets.

Obviously a woman who liked silver.

"Give me a hug," she said, taking a half step, half hop toward him. Travis backed up a full step. "Every-one needs a hug."

"Thanks, but I'm good."

"Poo, I wasn't going to hurt you. Just give you a hug. A big strong man like you, Travis Walker, shouldn't be afraid of an old woman."

Travis narrowed his eyes. "I'm not afraid of you. I just didn't want you to hurt yourself rushing like that."

The elderly woman laughed. "I'm not sure you remember me, but I'm Dani's grandmother, Freda. And by the way, double poo. You're not worried I'm going to break a hip. You're worried I'll get some old-lady cootie germs on you. You're too young to be afraid. You need to face those fears and over-come them."

Looking into her smiling face, he realized Dani had the exact same eyes as her grandmother. And just like her grandmother, Dani's eyes twinkled when she laughed.

"Fine." He leaned down and gave Dani's grandmother a light hug. "There," he said.

"Poo." She wrapped her arms around him and hugged so hard he was pretty sure she bruised a rib or two. "Now that's a hug. You're going to have to work on that."

She released Travis, then grabbed Dani's hand, tugging her into the house. As they went inside, he heard Freda say, "Dani, help Travis learn how to hug. He stinks at it."

DANI LED the way to the living room while her grandmother hurried away to get something or other. She deliberately didn't respond to her grandmother's order. She knew all too well that Travis didn't need any help when it came to hugging. He'd done a wonderful job when they'd hugged in his office. A little too wonderful.

He'd made her thoughts wander in a dangerous direction, something she couldn't afford at the moment. She didn't have time to have a hot-and-heavy affair. She'd worked too long and too hard to get distracted now.

So any temptation she might have felt in that direction went straight out the window when he'd looked at her lips the way he had. At first, she'd felt her skin tingle with awareness and her breath catch in her throat. But then, thankfully, sanity had returned, and she was proud of herself for telling him to stop it.

Sure, she was glad to see Travis. He was an old friend she'd hired to help her with a family problem. That was it. He'd help her prevent this lawsuit. Then they'd move on with their lives.

"What kind of insurance did you say your father sells?" Travis asked as he examined the room.

Dani never came in here, so she didn't really pay attention to the room. But now, taking in the obviously original artwork, the oversized, expensive furniture, and the ornate trimmings, she realized the room dripped money.

Her mother's doing. She'd hired the best decorator—which translated to most expensive—to make the house a showplace. Not one thing in this room reflected the personalities of the people who lived here.

"He's president of the company," she admitted.

Travis pulled out the little notepad she'd seen him tuck in his jacket pocket before they'd left his office.

"What are you doing?" she asked.

"Making a note to myself to become president of an insurance company."

Dani smiled, but only a little. "Being rich doesn't mean you're happy."

"But being poor doesn't mean you're happy either," he rebutted.

The look he gave her was filled with understanding, compassion and more than a little warmth. She glanced away and staunchly resisted the impulse to glance at him again. She'd always been a sucker for chocolate-brown hair and equally chocolate-brown eyes, the exact kind Travis had. She wondered why she'd never found herself attracted to him in high school. Maybe it was because, as she'd told him, she'd been too smart.

Unfortunately, she didn't seem too smart now. Desire spread through her every time he looked at her with those sexy eyes of his. Still, she wasn't eighteen anymore and sexy eyes didn't cut it now. By the time you reached twenty-eight, you needed more from a man than good looks and a great smile.

"Danielle, I see you're being insistent about this."

Dani turned and watched her mother's grand entrance. There was no other way to put it. The woman made it seem that there should be red carpet under her feet and trumpets heralding her arrival.

Deborah Karlinski turned to Travis, scanned him up and down, then said, "This is the detective, I take it. The one you went to school with."

Dani wouldn't have blamed Travis if he'd said something snide back, but instead, he extended his hand. "Yes, I'm Travis Walker, Mrs. Karlinski. It's nice to meet you."

Her mother took his hand with such reluctance you would have thought Travis was coated in mud.

"You're wasting your time," she told Travis. "I say we simply give the man the money he wants and move on with our lives. There's no sense splashing family business across the papers."

Dani knew that was the main reason her mother opposed this. She didn't want the embarrassment.

But Nana Freda had the right to handle the matter her own way, and Dani was all set to tell her mother that when her grandmother came into the room dragging a tea cart behind her. Travis immediately crossed the room and brought the cart over to the couch.

"Nana, why didn't you tell me you wanted tea?" Dani asked. "I would have gotten it for us."

"I'm not dead yet, so stop making me useless," her grandmother said. With a look at her daughter-in-law, she asked, "You want to stay and help with the plan?"

Dani's mother looked as if Freda had suggested she dance around the room in a chicken suit. With a loud "Ha," she left, disapproval trailing behind her.

"I love these special bonding moments with your mother," Freda quipped, sitting on the large white sofa. She looked at Travis. "Has Dani told you what I need?"

He nodded. "You want me to track down other people you've cursed and show that what you said didn't happen."

"First, they're not curses. I know Dani calls them that, but they are *romantic suggestions*. And second, of course they worked. Why would I give people romantic suggestions if they didn't work?" She gave Travis a look that made it fairly clear she wasn't too sure about him.

"I guess you wouldn't," Travis said. "Be a waste of time."

"Exactly. Now I'd like some tea," Freda said. "With four sugars."

Travis frowned. "Four? Isn't that a—"

"Interested in trying out one of my romantic suggestions yourself? We could see firsthand if it works."

Dani bit back a smile. Poor Trav. The women in her family weren't treating him very well. Her mother didn't like him; her grandmother was talking to him as if he were a fairly dim lightbulb.

And she herself had treated him a little harshly. Because of her own wayward thoughts, she'd overreacted to the look he'd given her. She shouldn't have gotten so mad at him when in actuality she was mad at herself.

"I'll help," she said, crossing the room to where Travis had placed the cart. Dani was all set to pour the tea, but by the time she got there, Travis was done.

"Nice," she commented.

"One of the advantages to living all over the world is that you become pretty adept at doing things. For your information, pouring tea into a cup is something I've mastered."

Dani smiled at his nonsense. Behind her, she heard her grandmother make a huffing-grunting noise, which was her way of laughing without letting anyone know she was laughing.

Dani glanced at Travis to see if he'd noticed, and he had a deep frown on his face.

"Is she choking?" he asked softly.

"No. Trying to mask her laughter."

Travis's frown deepened. "Sure sounds like a near-death noise to me."

"What are you two whispering about? If it has to do with this silly lawsuit, then I need to hear it, too," Freda insisted.

Dani was going to take the teacup to her grandmother, but Travis beat her to it. He carried it across the room and placed it next to the elderly woman.

"We weren't talking about the case," he said. "You made an odd noise, and I was asking Dani if you were okay."

Wow, talk about direct. Dani waited to see what her grandmother would do. Freda might look sweet and kind, but she had a temper.

For a second or two, it seemed as though her temper was going to get the better of her. Then, surprisingly, Freda laughed. Not the muffled huffing-grunting noise she'd used before, but a good, old-fashioned belly laugh.

"You're something else," Freda told Travis.

"But you're just not sure what that something else is," he countered.

Freda laughed again, and Dani smiled. Travis had broken through to the older woman in record time. Most people never impressed Freda to the point where she'd relax around them.

But she sure seemed to like Travis.

"You're funny," Freda said. "And I have a good feeling about you. I bet you can help me with this case."

"I think I can." Travis sat down next to Dani's grandmother. "Why don't you tell me about these curses?"

"Romantic suggestions," Freda corrected.

"Right. Romantic suggestions. Why do you do it?"

Freda leaned toward him, her expression intense as she said, "People should be nicer. And when they're not, I know it's because something is wrong with their love life. So I help them have a better love life, which in turn makes them nicer to people like me."

Travis nodded. "I see. And you're convinced these work."

"I *know* they work." She looked at Dani. "And don't start with that whole power-of-suggestion thing again. My suggestions work because *I* have a power."

"A power?" Travis glanced at Dani and raised one eyebrow. Before she could say anything in her grandmother's defense, the older woman tapped him on the arm.

"Yes, a power. Not something like the ability to see through walls or run as fast as cars. No, my power is much more profound than that. I can make people have a happy love life, and there's no more potent power in the whole world."

Her grandmother leaned back against the sofa and gave Travis a pointed look. "Too many people dismiss the power of love, but it is all that truly matters in this world."

Dani had heard her grandmother's philosophy many times while growing up. She knew Nana Freda did it to temper the other message that was constantly sent by her parents—that what mattered was success, and success was measured by the size of a paycheck. Her father certainly didn't believe in love despite growing up with a mother who was interested only in love. And with each passing year, her mother became more and more obsessed with image and status.

"Nana, you're a romantic," Dani said.

"Love is everything," her grandmother pronounced.

"Sure is important," Travis agreed. "Keeps the population growing."

"Poo." Freda waved one hand and made her bracelets jangle. "That's not love. That's monkey business. I'm talking about love, which is something a young man like you probably tries to avoid."

"I've dodged it so far." Travis flashed Freda a grin, and Dani watched as her grandmother fell under the spell of that grin. She'd give Travis that, he did have a way with women.

"You should try it. Love makes you happy," Freda repeated.

"I'm not really the settle-down kind." Travis looked at Dani. "What about you?"

Dani laughed and admitted, "Love is the last thing I'm interested in at the moment. It's taken me too long to get where I am to lose focus now."

"You two are sad," Freda said. "Really sad." Then brightening, she added, "Perhaps I could use my power to help you—"

"No, Nana."

"Don't."

Dani looked at Travis, who'd spoken at the same time she had. "Guess we both believe in your spells just a little."

"Hey, I'm not taking any chances," Travis said. He pulled his notebook from his shirt pocket. "Back to the case and people who weren't as fortunate as Dani and me. Do you remember the names of anyone you cursed?"

"They are not curses," Freda said.

"Okay, people you've given romantic suggestions to," he said. "Do you remember them?"

Freda fumbled in the pocket of her dress, then pulled out a large roll of paper with three rubber-bands around it. "Here are the names."

Travis took the roll. "Big list," he said dryly.

"Nana Freda, you've cursed that many people?" Dani stared at the roll. It was huge.

"They are *not* curses," her grandmother said. "But yes, I have helped many people find love."

Travis glanced at Dani, and she could tell he was thinking the same thing she was thinking. Based on the size of this list, her grandmother was lucky no one else had sued her before now.

"I'll take this back to the office and start tracking down some of these people," Travis said.

"You're going to find them happy." Her grandmother had a cat-who-ate-the-canary smile on her face. "Carl Whitley would have been happy, too, if he hadn't misinterpreted my romantic suggestion. He was dense, which is why I'm not giving him a dime of my money."

"How did he react when you made your romantic suggestion?" Travis asked. He glanced at Dani, then back at her grandmother. "What was it? That love would overwhelm him?"

"Yes. That's what I said." She straightened her shawl around her shoulders. "He was being very nasty to everyone, so I knew he was having problems with his love life."

"He's seventy-two," Dani said.

"So? That doesn't mean he's too old for a love life. I'm seventy-one, and I still have a love life."

Travis looked downright skeptical, and Dani bit back a laugh. Her grandmother had gone on one date two years ago. That hardly qualified as a love life.

Although come to think of it, Dani couldn't remember the last time she'd been on a date either.

Travis obviously decided to avoid the topic. Instead, he asked, "So what did he say when you made your romantic suggestion?"

"He laughed at me," Freda admitted, smiling. "I thought that was cute, that he would laugh like that. I knew he didn't believe me, but at least it made him happy. And I knew that soon he would believe."

Travis wrote something down. "Why did you choose that particular suggestion?"

She leaned forward and said slowly, "Because he needed a lot of love."

"I see. And when you made this romantic suggestion, did you just say it, or did you do something else?"

Freda frowned at him. "What? Like a dance or something?"

Travis shot a quick, conspiratorial look at Dani, then he asked, "Did you point one finger at him?"

Dani opened her mouth to say of course her grandmother hadn't when Nana Freda said, "Naturally."

Dani frowned. "You did?"

"Of course."

"So you do point at people and then say the romantic suggestion." Travis shook his head. "I've got to tell you, Freda, it sure does sound like a curse."

"I have to point so the suggestion lands on the right person," her grandmother reasoned. "If I didn't, it might hit someone else by mistake."

Dani was half-afraid to ask the question that suddenly occurred to her, but she had no choice. "Tell me you don't squint or make some sort of evil face, too."

Nana Freda tipped her chin and looked hurt. "I would never squint at someone. I look at them intensely and speak very clearly, that's all."

"While pointing," Travis added.

"Yes. While pointing." Her grandmother smiled. "See, there's nothing remotely curse-like about it."

Dani couldn't believe it. All those poor people. Surely they'd felt as if they'd been cursed by a crazy woman.

She looked at Travis and saw he was fighting not to laugh. She needed to get him out of here now.

"Thanks for the information, Nana. I'm sure Travis will be able to find several people to talk to in the next couple of days."

"Carl should have used his brain," her grandmother said. "He shouldn't have taken up with that floozy. She only wanted his money. She didn't truly love him."

"Do you think he truly loved her?" Dani asked.

Her grandmother shook her head. "No. She was not the one I meant the suggestion for. Carl just misunderstood."

Regardless of whom her grandmother had meant Carl Whitley to fall for, Dani knew they were going to have a tough battle on their hands. The lawyer Carl had hired was good. The only glimmer of hope Dani had was that Carl's lawyer had suggested they talk before an actual suit was filed. Dani had jumped at the chance, and she hoped that when they had this meeting, she'd have some strong evidence to back her side up.

Travis stood. "I'll start tracking down some of these people."

"I want Dani to go with you when you talk to them," her grandmother said, folding her hands in her lap. "Family should be there."

Oh, no. No, no. This wouldn't work at all. "I can't. I have to get ready to move to New York, Nana, re-member," Dani asked. "Besides, Travis can talk to these people on the phone."

Her grandmother frowned. "You said you would help me."

"I am helping. I've hired Travis." Dani looked at Travis for backing. "He doesn't need me."

"I can take care of this," Travis assured the older woman.

Although her grandmother was small, she suddenly didn't seem so. She straightened, and then looked Dani dead in the eyes. It was an intense look. An unnerving look.

"I want my granddaughter to meet these people. I want a member of my family to see that I have done these people no harm."

Dani considered arguing, but she wasn't that brave—or that foolish. She could tell how much this meant to her grandmother. Reluctantly, she said, "Fine. I'll go with Travis and meet the people."

Immediately, Nana Freda's expression changed. She grinned and clapped her hands. "Perfect. The two of you doing this together will be perfect."

Dani looked at Travis, who shrugged, and then she looked back at her grandmother, who seemed way too happy. Dani didn't like that smile on her grandmother's face one bit. The woman was up to something.

No doubt about it.

3

TRAVIS GLANCED over at Dani in the passenger's seat
of his car then quickly refocused on the road. Man,
she looked terrific today. The dark jeans and pale-
blue T-shirt she had on made it difficult—no make
that almost impossible—for him to keep his attention
on the road. Where was a cold shower when you really needed one?

The second he'd seen her this afternoon, he'd
known he was in deep trouble, but what could he do?
He couldn't refuse to let her come with him. For starters, her grandmother had insisted. Then, there was
the fact that she'd cheerfully met him at his office at
one, just as she'd promised. As she'd stood there,
smiling at him, looking so sexy he'd started to sweat,
he'd tried to come up with a single reasonable excuse
why she shouldn't come with him.

And promptly drawn a blank.

So now, ten minutes later, they were on the road,
off to meet their first curse recipient, Peggy Law-
rence, a friend from high school. At least this meeting should be easy. Peggy had said on the phone that

not only did she not remember the curse, she only vaguely remembered Dani's grandmother.

Maybe they could wrap this up quickly. The sooner he put this case behind him, the happier he'd be. This attraction thing with Dani bugged him. He'd been hoping that when he saw her today the sizzle dancing between them would be gone.

But no such luck. Right now, lust was coiled around him like a serpent.

This was *not* good. Dani was a friend. Dani was a client. Dani wasn't supposed to be the object of lust.

But looking at her now, the sun making her dark hair shine, the faint scent of her perfume filling his lungs, he had to admit the blatantly obvious…

His old friend from high school turned him on big-time.

"How's your brother doing?" Dani asked.

Travis welcomed the excuse to think about anything but how sexy she looked.

"Max is good. Got married two weeks ago, so at the moment, he's basking in the joy of new love."

"Um, mind if I point out that you sound a tad cynical there, old friend," she said, humor tainting her voice. "Why? Is it love in general you don't like or is it the woman Max married?"

Travis shrugged. "I think Paige is great. She's perfect for Max. And he's perfect for her," he admitted. "Max is the type who is suited to being married, so the two of them probably will be blissfully happy. But for the most part, I think people expect too much from something that's really just chemistry."

"Interesting theory," she said. "How so?"

He couldn't tell if Dani was simply humoring him or if she sincerely wanted to hear his opinion. As much to himself as to her, he explained, "Let's face it—people wrap emotions around what is actually only sexual attraction and expect it to last forever. It's all a big marketing ploy to get people to spend their money. You need to buy cards and flowers and gifts for this person. You need to go to expensive, romantic restaurants with this person. You spend a fortune marrying this person. It's just sex. Sure, for a while, it can be amazing. But eventually, it fades and what are you left with? A big, fat credit-card bill."

He hadn't meant to be so vehement, but he'd warmed to his topic. He knew she was going to argue with him. She couldn't possibly agree with everything he'd just said. Hell, he didn't really agree with absolutely everything he'd just said either. He'd gotten caught up in his subject and taken it a little further than he'd meant to.

But basically, he believed most of what he'd said, so he waited for her reaction. He looked over at Dani, who had a thoughtful, almost pensive, expression on her face as if she were seriously considering his side.

Finally, she slowly nodded. "Good point. Romance is hooey. Sex rules. People should have sex a few times, and when it gets boring, move on. Life would be so much simpler if you could have some fun, and then when you needed to move on, just say, 'It was great, but I'm out of here' without the other person getting hurt."

Travis stared at her, stunned. "That's not quite what I meant. Do you really feel that way?" he finally managed to ask.

"Sure. Why not? I'd never given it a lot of thought before, but you make a valid point. Look at the man suing my grandmother. If Carl hadn't gotten so blinded by what he thought was love, his business wouldn't have suffered, and my grandmother wouldn't have gotten into trouble. See, life would have been simpler. The man made his mistake by thinking it was love and that love lasts forever."

Not to play devil's advocate since she was on his side, but Travis couldn't help but point out, "For *most* people it doesn't last, but I guess there are some people who stay together forever."

Dani shook her head. "Don't water down your theory. Let's face it, if they stay together, it's probably not because they're wildly in love. They probably stay together because of the kids, or the finances or because it's a nice routine. My parents have been married for over thirty years, and I can guarantee you, love has nothing to do with them still being together."

Travis frowned and tapped one hand on the steering wheel. Funny, when he said he didn't believe in love, it made sense. But it bugged him when she said it. It sounded harsh. And sad. How insane could he get? He didn't mind that he didn't believe in love, but it bothered him that she didn't?

He glanced once more at her, trying to judge if Dani really believed what she was saying. After a couple of seconds, he admitted defeat. He couldn't read her like he'd been able to when they'd been teens. She had her lawyer face on and he had no idea if she was serious or just playing with him.

"What makes you dislike love?" he asked. "Did something happen to make you cynical?"

Dani laughed. "Okay, Trav, I'm confused. I'm *agreeing* with you. Love is overrated."

Travis knew he was coming across like a lunatic, but he couldn't help it. Dani had always been an optimist in high school, so he couldn't help wondering what had happened during the last ten years to change her.

"Did you get your heart broken? Is that why you're so down on love?" he persisted.

Dani laughed again and whacked him lightly on the arm. "You need to be locked up."

"I'm just curious. I've never been in love or thought I was in love. Plus, I was never a romantic kind of guy, so it makes sense I'd feel the way I do."

"You need a padded room and some soft pillows," she continued.

Yeah, she was right. He was the official poster boy for the love-is-hype camp, so he should be thrilled that Dani shared his opinion.

Man, he was really losing it.

"I can view love from an intellectual standpoint," he said, and immediately realized his mistake.

"And I can't take an intellectual approach to a topic like love?" she asked before he could back-pedal.

"Well sure. But you're a…"

Dani narrowed her eyes and in that split second, Travis knew why she was good in court. That look could melt paint off a car. "Be really careful what you say next, Killer."

"You're an optimist," he said, which seemed to placate her somewhat. "You think the best about everyone and everything."

"For starters, I'm not an optimist anymore. These days, I firmly reside in the realist camp. You don't spend your days defending corporate executives who've dipped into the company cookie jar to buy themselves expensive doodads and remain an optimist for long. And secondly, I can view love from an intellectual standpoint just like you can."

She had a good point. It was easy to be an optimist when you were young. Still, it made him sad to think life had taken the sheen off the world for her.

"So you've never been in love?" he asked.

She shrugged. "Doesn't matter if I have."

Travis headed toward the freeway and laughed. "Oh yes it does. The way it works is that if you've thought you were in love at some point, you've got the virus. Once you've been bitten, you tend to have that emotional stuff running through your veins your whole life."

Dani laughed again, the sound light and free in his small car. "It's a good thing you're not a lawyer, Travis. Your logic is so convoluted even you can't follow it."

Knowing she was right, he chuckled. "Yeah, I am getting twisted up here, aren't I?"

"You're a regular pretzel. So why don't we both settle for agreeing that neither one of us is a big believer in happily-ever-after, but that we both hope things work out well for Max and his new wife."

Travis nodded. "Yeah, Max is different. He believes in love, and I think it's kind of like those curses your grandmother hands out. If you sincerely believe in something, maybe that's enough to make it true. Max sincerely believes in what he feels for Paige, and that's probably enough for it to last."

"I guess time will tell."

"Guess so."

For a while, they drove in silence, and then Dani asked, "What about Peggy? Does Peggy remember the curse?"

"No. She was happy to hear from me, but she didn't have a clue what I was talking about when I brought up the curse."

"That could work in our favor. Here's a woman whose life hasn't been impacted a bit by what Nana said. I think our day will turn out to be a productive one."

Travis glanced again at Dani and debated about the next question he wanted to ask. But he had to know what was going on. It bothered him that her grandmother had insisted that Dani come along. He didn't want either woman getting the wrong idea about his talent as a detective. He was surprised how much it bothered him that Dani might think he was clueless.

"I can do this alone," he qualified, then frowned at his own stupidity. Way to be suave, Walker. Just blurt stuff out like a four-year-old.

Dani had been looking out the side window, but now she glanced at him. "Well, good. I'm glad you can drive by yourself," she said slowly, obviously baffled by his statement. "I'm hoping you can also dress and feed yourself."

He took the exit off the freeway and stopped at a red light, then said bluntly, "I'm a good private investigator."

Dani nodded slowly. "I assumed so or I wouldn't have hired you."

Deciding to give this one last shot, he asked the question that had been bothering him since they'd spoken to Freda yesterday. "Not that I mind the company, because I don't, but could you explain why it was so important to your grandmother that you come along with me? Doesn't she trust me?"

For a second, Dani didn't say a word. Then she burst out laughing.

Okay, that wasn't quite the reaction he'd expected. He waited patiently until she got herself under control.

"Glad I amuse you," he said dryly once her giggles had become hiccups.

She patted his arm. "Oh, Trav, you know I'm not laughing *at* you."

"I do, do I?"

"Yes. Or at least you should. You met my grandmother. You know this has nothing to do with your skill as a detective, so don't pout."

"Hey, I'm *not* pouting. Just concerned. So if it's not about my skill, then what does it have to do with? This is overkill, having both of us visit Peggy. In fact, there's really no reason for me to meet these people in person unless you want depositions. If all you want to know is if the curse changed their lives, I can ask that on the phone."

Dani shook her head and shifted in her seat so she was half facing him. "You're looking at this all wrong. You and I are trying to accomplish one thing, and I'm pretty sure my grandmother is trying to accomplish something completely different."

Travis frowned, not liking the sound of this. "Such as?"

"The woman is a hopeless romantic who desperately wishes her only grandchild was married with a couple of children. I think this whole scheme of insisting I go with you is just her way of matchmaking."

Travis didn't like the sound of that, especially considering the level of attraction he felt toward Dani.

"You don't—" he started, but she laughed.

"No, I'm *definitely* not interested in her matchmaking plans. We've already agreed to keep things on a friends-only level."

She sounded so adamant that Travis relaxed. "I don't remember us making that agreement, but it sounds like a good one."

Dani nodded. "It's the only smart thing to do."

"Yeah, and rumor has it you're very smart," he teased as he turned onto a tree-lined street with tidy, two-story houses.

"This neighborhood seems nice," Dani said. "Peggy must be doing okay. What did Nana say to her?"

Travis parked in front of a red brick house with white shutters. "Freda said that Peggy would have love in abundance."

"What does that mean?"

"You're asking me? She's your grandmother. I figure it means Peggy's been married and divorced a dozen times." He shoved open his door. "Want to go find out?"

Dani nodded. "Absolutely. I have a really good feeling about this."

EVERY OUNCE of good feeling Dani had shriveled up the second the front door opened. Peggy stood framed in the entrance, still as tall and redheaded as she'd been in high school. That part didn't surprise Dani, nor was she surprised that Peggy still had a big smile and a loud laugh.

No, what stomped Dani's hopes into the ground

were the children surrounding Peggy. Not just one or
two. But a whole flock of them.

"Wow, Peggy, are all these children yours?" Dani
asked, following the other woman into the house.

"Yep. Stan and I have seven." She grinned. "Guess
he and I can't seem to figure out what's causing it."

Dani watched as a little girl wrapped her arms
around Peggy's leg and started sucking her thumb.

Dani barely kept her mouth from falling open.
Seven children? Peggy had seven children?

Nana Freda's words ran through Dani's mind.
She'd told Peggy she would have love in abundance.
Dani surveyed the crowd of redheaded, freckled
faces. Boy, this sure looked like abundance to her.

"It's so great to see you both," Peggy said, leading the way to a living room filled with toys. She sat
on a worn brown couch and smiled. "I have my
hands filled, so I don't get to catch up with high-
school friends."

Dani slowly sank into one of the chairs facing the
couch, then glanced at Travis. He looked as stunned
as she felt.

"Hey, Peggy, I didn't know you wanted so many
kids," Travis said, leaning down and straightening a
toddler who was wobbling toward the wall. "Hold
up there, buddy. You're about to crash."

Peggy laughed. "Me? Want a lot of children? No
way. I was going to be a career woman and conquer
Madison Avenue. I never thought for a second I'd be a
housewife, let alone a housewife with a brood this big."

"Mama says we're her angels." A little girl plopped onto the sofa and cuddled against her mother. "She likes angels."

Peggy gathered the girl close and gave her several loud, smacking kisses. "Yes, I do. And angels you are. Angels sent from heaven to make me smile."

The little girl giggled as her mother kissed her cheeks, and Dani couldn't help smiling. Peggy might not have planned to be a mom, but she sure was a great one. Although the family didn't seem to have a lot in the way of possessions, Dani literally could feel the love in this house.

She looked over at Travis, who was steering yet another youngster away from trouble. He must have sensed her gaze because he abruptly turned his head and looked at her. The sight of that handsome, virile man helping two little children made the breath catch in Dani's throat.

Just as she had yesterday, she felt attraction dance between them. Alive. Vibrant. Intense. For a moment, she simply stared at Travis, lost in his gaze, lost in the heat she saw slowly build there.

Then the sound of Peggy's laughter shattered the spell like fine crystal hitting stone.

"I've been trying to remember this whole curse thing since you called, Travis, but I keep drawing a blank," Peggy said. "All I vaguely remember is making Dani's grandmother mad one night when we brought Dani home late and made a lot of noise dropping her off. Her grandmother yelled something out the window, but I haven't a clue what."

Dani hated what she had to say, but she felt she owed it to Peggy. "My grandmother said you would have love in abundance."

"Love in abundance," Peggy repeated slowly.

The words seemed to hover in the room, and despite the number of rowdy children, the air felt silent. Heavy.

Peggy sat perfectly still for a moment as her children played around her. Dani watched as the other woman scanned the living room, almost as if she were seeing it for the first time. Tension coiled within Dani as she waited for Peggy's reaction.

No one could look around this house and not realize the curse had indeed come true.

"Think how sad your life would be if you didn't have your children," Travis said softly. "Think how empty you'd feel."

The truth of Travis's words was obvious to all of them, and Dani wanted to kiss him for pointing out what was so blatantly right. Peggy did belong here with these children.

A big smile formed on the other woman's face. "I would be miserable without my children. My life would be nothing."

"We're her angels," the little girl repeated.

"Absolutely." Turning to Dani, Peggy added, "I don't know if my family has anything to do with your grandmother and what she said to me, but if so, then it wasn't a curse. It was a blessing."

Dani returned Peggy's smile. Although finding Peggy like this wouldn't help their case, Dani was glad she was happy.

"I honestly don't think what my grandmother said all those years ago has anything to do with your family, but I'll tell her just the same. She likes to believe her little romantic suggestions come true, so it will make her happy to think it made you happy."

"And we are happy. These kids may be a handful, but I wouldn't trade them for all the high-powered New York City jobs in the world." Peggy kissed her daughter's head. "Stan and I are truly lucky, and it seems like we may have your grandmother to thank."

TRAVIS GLANCED at his watch as they headed back to his car. They'd ended up spending almost three hours visiting with Peggy and her children. It had been fun, but man, seven kids sure could wear you out. He had no idea how Peggy and her husband kept up with them.

"Well, we certainly can't use her," Dani said, as she snapped her seat belt shut. "Talk about a curse that came true."

"She's happy. Maybe you could use that in your favor. You know, point out that even though what your grandmother said would happen did happen, Peggy is delighted."

"And living a life that may be the direct result of my grandmother's romantic suggestion." Dani sighed. "I'll get laughed at if I bring in Peggy."

Yeah, she probably had a point there. Peggy did seem to make a great case for the other side.

"It's a coincidence," he said. "She didn't even remember what your grandmother said, so it's not like the power of suggestion was at work."

"I think that makes it worse. If I could use the power-of-suggestion defense, then I could say Carl didn't have to believe what Nana said would happen. But Peggy didn't even hear her, so there's no way the power of suggestion was at work."

Left with no clue what to say that might make her feel better, Travis suggested, "Since there's nothing we can do about it right now, let's go to dinner. I bet you haven't been to Bernie's for pizza in years."

That cheered her up. Dani immediately smiled. "Bernie's is still in business?"

"Of course it's still in business. It's not like the people of Chicago have forgotten what good pizza tastes like. We'll be lucky if we can find a place to sit."

"Yeah, right." She rolled her eyes. "I doubt it's going to be so busy that we'll end up sitting at one of the cement tables outside. I think there'll be room for us."

"Want to bet?" he teased.

Dani took him up on it. "Absolutely. I'll bet you that we'll have no problem getting a place to sit at Bernie's. Loser pays for dinner."

"Sounds good," he said, and bit back a grin.

Then he didn't say another word. Not as he drove to Bernie's Pizzeria. Not as they stood in the long,

long line to place their order and the equally long, long line to pick up their order. Not as Dani paid for their pizza and soda.

And not as they both sat at one of the cement tables scattered in front of the small restaurant.

Instead, he did the gentlemanly thing and didn't point out to Dani that he'd been right and she'd been wrong.

"You can stop smirking now," she said, taking a slice of the thick cheesy pizza. "I underestimated the lasting appeal of Bernie's."

Travis grinned. "Some things just get better with age, and Bernie's is one of those things."

With a glance at their surroundings, Dani said dryly, "I imagine it's the ambiance that pulls them in."

Travis chuckled. "Don't be a snob. The food is great. The place is fun. People come here with their friends to hang out, just like we did in high school."

"So you still come here?"

"Sometimes. Not as often as we did when we were young, but that's not because I don't want to. It's because I'm busy these days." He took a bite of his pizza and watched her do the same. Her blissful expression made it clear she was rediscovering the joys of Bernie's pizza.

"This is amazing," she said once she'd swallowed. "I'd completely forgotten."

He loved the happy look on her face. At this moment, with the cool night air surrounding them and the expression on Dani's face, Travis felt young again.

He felt like the eighteen-year-old kid who loved to spend time with his friends, just laughing and joking and being alive.

"You don't get a chance to relax often, do you?" he asked, already knowing the answer.

"Does anyone once they're grown up and having to scramble to build a career?" She took another bite of pizza and made a sexy noise that really set Travis's blood pounding hard through his body.

To distract himself, he said, "I try to enjoy life, too. I make sure I leave myself downtime."

"If you give yourself too much downtime, you won't have much of a career," she pointed out.

"But you'll be happy."

"Not if being successful is what you really want out of life."

"Touché. You've got me there." He flashed her a grin. "Guess I'm still a lazy kid at heart. I'll leave conquering the world to you."

"I don't want to conquer the world," she said, but the tiny smile she had belied her words. When he raised one eyebrow and gave her a dubious look, she laughed. "Okay, maybe I want to conquer a small part of it. But not all of it."

"Oh, well, in that case, you're practically a lazy kid, too."

She laughed, and put her hand on his arm. He liked the feel of her touching him, and once again, he felt desire flare within him.

"You can't be too lazy. I bet you worked hard when you were in the navy," she said.

He tried to think about her comment, but the only thoughts crowding into his brain were about all the things he'd like to do with and to Dani.

When she repeated her comment, he said, "That's why I got out. I didn't like having to jump when someone told me to jump."

"Ah, an independent soul," she said, and then she flexed her fingers across his skin, caressing him lightly.

Her expression was completely innocent, but there was nothing innocent about her touch. He could have let it go and pretended it wasn't happening, but that probably wasn't the smartest thing for either of them.

"To quote you, stop it," he said, moving his arm away. "If I don't get to give you sexy looks, then you don't get to caress my arm."

She opened her mouth, no doubt to protest, but immediately shut it and nodded.

"You're right. Fair is fair." Gathering up her trash, she walked over and tossed it in the big metal garbage can tucked under a tree. "I guess we should head back to your office now so I can get my car."

Travis followed her, feeling half like a jerk and half like a hero. On the one hand, he hadn't meant to upset her, but on the other hand, he was only human.

They were both quiet on the ride back to his office. She was probably feeling the way he felt, that if things were different, something definitely would happen between them. Desire again surrounded them, and it took a hell of a lot of self-control to ignore it.

But he did. He didn't do or say a thing that would give in to the lust he felt burning hot within him for Dani. Instead, he played it cool. He parked near her car and turned off the engine.

"Are you coming with me tomorrow when I interview the next person?" he asked, figuring she'd say no.

"Of course I am." She shoved open her car door and was half out when she added, "Oh, and I'm sorry about tonight. I'm usually smarter than that."

Before he could say a thing, she was out of his car and heading toward hers. Travis climbed out, intending to stop her but then realized he shouldn't. It was better this way.

So he stood near the back of his car and watched her unlock her door. She seemed cool and calm, but he'd bet his Bulls season tickets that was all an act.

"Have a good night," she said, opening her car door. She dropped her things inside, climbed in, then buckled her seat belt. After a second, Travis noticed something was wrong, because she started muttering and mumbling.

"Don't say a word," she told him.

Travis bit back a smile. Yeah, she was far from calm. "Hey, I can be uncoordinated, too. What did you do?"

"Nothing. And don't talk," she said, which only made him laugh more.

"Seriously, let me help you." He took a step forward, but she once again told him to stay where he was. After a minute, he figured it was safe to get closer, and when he did, he saw she'd caught her T-shirt in her seat belt.

"Need some help?" he asked, leaning inside her car a little.

Dani immediately leaned away from him. "What are you doing?"

"Helping." He hunkered next to her seat. She'd smashed the buckle of the seatbelt into the lock and jammed a big chunk of her T-shirt in with it.

"I hope this doesn't tear," he said, slowly moving her hands away. "It's a nice T-shirt."

Dani kept fiddling with the belt and the shirt, and no matter how many times he tried to help, she just kept saying she had it.

Finally he sighed. "You're going to ruin your shirt."

Turning her head, Dani looked at him. He tried to read her expression, tried to tell what she was thinking, and at first, he couldn't.

Then he saw the fire. Burning deep within her amazing black eyes was a heat like none he'd ever seen. Desire had caught her in its spell just as it had him, and she was feeling the same undertow of attraction that he was feeling.

"I should leave," she said softly, her gaze never leaving his.

"Yes," he said, reaching out and touching her cheek gently. "You should leave."

Her gaze moved to his lips, and Travis felt the air whoosh from his lungs. Damn, she looked as hungry as he felt, and he found himself moving closer.

"I really, *really* should leave," she said, but her words were meaningless since she was still staring at his lips.

"Yes." He brushed the hair off her face. "Leaving would be the smart thing to do."

"And I'm very smart," she answered. She met his gaze once more, and a teasing, tempting smile formed on her lips. "Or at least, I used to be."

Then, with a little murmur of defeat, she kissed him.

4

THE FIRST THING that occurred to Dani as she kissed Travis was that he was a wonderful kisser. Really. A truly first-class, knock-your-socks off, melt-you-into-a-puddle kisser.

And the second thing that occurred to her was she was a fool. What intelligent woman kissed Travis Walker? It was as foolish as standing under a tree during a lightning storm. Something bad was bound to happen.

She pondered that while she tipped her head and continued to kiss him. Travis kissed just as she'd known he would—with finesse. He used just enough pressure to curl her toes. Girls had talked in high school about how talented he was, and she could now personally testify that yes, the man had talent.

"You're thinking about the kiss," he murmured against her lips. "I can almost hear your brain whirling around in there."

Dani didn't want the kiss to end yet. Despite the whole foolish factor, she was enjoying herself immensely. "Um, no."

He nibbled on the corner of her mouth. "Um, yes."

She smiled, and typical of sneaky Travis Walker, he took advantage of the situation. He slid the tip of his tongue along the inside of her bottom lip, effectively finding a way to get her to stop thinking about anything but him.

Dani wrapped her arms around his neck and turned herself over to the kiss. If she was going to be foolish, this certainly was a pleasant way to accomplish it.

She had no idea how long she sat in her car kissing Travis, but she didn't regret a second of it. In fact, the only regret she had was when he finally broke off the kiss and looked at her in the dim light from the interior of her car.

"That was nice," he said, his deep voice washing over Dani like warm water.

"Yes." For a second, she considered him and debated what else to say. Common sense told her she should explain all the reasons why they shouldn't have kissed, but right at this moment, she was simply too happy to do that.

Instead, she decided to leave well enough alone. Travis was a smart guy. He knew they couldn't get involved. He didn't need her to point out the blatantly obvious to him.

For once she decided not to analyze a situation to death and instead just accept it. She flashed Travis a smile, put the key in her car's ignition, and said, "I guess I'll see you in the morning. We still need one or two good curse recipients to convince Carl Whitley not to file this suit."

Dani knew Travis had expected her to do a postmortem on the kiss, and he seemed really happy she wasn't. He stood and said, "Okay. Meet you here at ten. Drive safely."

With that, he shut the driver's door to her car, and walked away. Dani watched him go. This whole not-talking-things-over had some definite upsides. They'd avoided any scenes, any melodrama.

They'd shared a kiss. Big deal. They'd both ignore that it had happened and simply go on with their lives.

Yeah, right.

THE NEXT MORNING, Travis glanced over at Dani as they walked across the campus of Grayton College and couldn't help wondering what was going on. Since when didn't women want to talk about things like kisses? What was up with Dani?

She seemed extremely happy this morning and hadn't mentioned the searing kiss they'd shared the night before. What about the agreement they'd had to just be friends? Didn't she want to discuss that?

Man, he was losing it. He should be happy she wanted to let it go. He certainly didn't want to talk about the kiss. What guy ever wanted to talk about things like that?

But since when didn't a woman want to dissect it to pieces?

"Did you get a chance to explain to Dr. Knightly

what we wanted to see him about?" Dani asked, not a trace of discomfort in her tone.

Travis pulled his mind back to the subject at hand. Today, they were meeting with another of Freda's curse recipients—Dr. Andrew Knightly. He taught in the psychology department at Grayton College and had told Travis during their phone conversation that he didn't believe in things like curses and spells.

"Yes, he knows we're coming and he guarantees that your grandmother had no impact on his life." Travis stopped and looked at the signs pointing to the various buildings. Why was it that colleges had the most complicated building names?

"He said he's in B45-12." Travis walked over to the campus map hanging in a display case outside what looked to be the student union. "I think it's that way," he said, pointing left.

Dani leaned around him and looked at the map, too. She brushed against his arm as she moved, and just like that, memories of last night's kiss slammed into his brain.

Man, it had been one spectacular kiss. He hadn't really expected it to rock his world the way it had. He'd always liked Dani, but he'd never expected them to share the kind of chemistry they'd experienced last night.

Not that she seemed overly impressed by it.

"No, I think the psych building is to the right," she said, pointing away from where they were standing.

"No, it's not." He nodded at the map. "The bookstore is directly behind us, so in that case, the psych building has to be to the left."

Dani tipped her head, the gesture making her look downright irresistible. "I think you're wrong."

"Hey, who's the private detective here?" Travis asked. "Figuring things out is what I do for a living. I think if I can solve intricate cases, I can read one little map. You have to learn to trust me."

Dani laughed, and Travis had to admit, he really liked that sound. She had a great laugh, rich and full and vibrant. It wasn't that feigned polite kind of laugh a lot of women used. When Dani laughed, he knew she meant it.

"Did I accidentally insult your deductive powers?" She had a definite twinkle in her eyes. "Sorry about that. Don't want to cause any lasting psychological damage." With a wink she added, "But if I do, maybe the psychologist we're going to meet can help you. Arrange for some therapy. Stuff like that."

"I'll keep it in mind," he said, leaning closer to the map. It was the worse drawing he'd ever seen. None of the buildings looked like what they were. Plus, according to the map, Dani and he were standing in the middle of a lake rather than on a sidewalk.

To find this building, he didn't need to be a detective, he needed to be a psychic.

"So which way do we go, oh mighty leader?" Dani asked.

Travis chuckled. "Cute."

"Why, thank you. I think you're cute, too."

She sure was in a playful mood this morning. He couldn't help wondering if the kiss they'd shared had anything to do with it. He knew it couldn't be the progress they were making on the case because they weren't making any.

"Apology accepted," he said, and then nodded toward the left. His gut told him to go that way. "The psych building is over there."

Dani looked dubious, but said, "Okay, I guess there's only one way to find out."

Making certain he didn't show her any of the uncertainty he was feeling, he led the way. Okay, so he wasn't one-hundred-percent certain they were going in the right direction, but he wasn't about to admit that to Dani. A guy had to have some dignity.

Thankfully, after they'd passed four large white buildings, they came to a smaller brown and beige building labeled Psychology. Travis didn't even try not to grin.

"Did I tell you I was a good detective or what?" he asked.

Dani laughed. "I can't believe you found it. Well, that proves I hired the right man for this case. I mean, if you can find a clearly marked four-story building in the middle of the day when surrounded by maps, then you can find anything."

Travis waved one hand toward the building. "Like I said, you've got to learn to trust me."

He was smiling as he followed Dani inside the

building. No two ways about it, he was going to miss her once she moved away. Looking back, he guessed he should have tried harder to stay in touch with the gang from high school. Sure, they'd all grown up and gotten busy, but that was just an excuse. Friends were friends, and he should try to hold on to the true ones.

True ones like Dani.

"I can't believe this man doesn't hate my grandmother," Dani said.

They'd reached the elevator, and while they waited, Travis pulled out the small notebook he carried. He scanned the notes he'd made when he'd talked to Dr. Knightly.

"Didn't seem to hold any resentment against Freda. In fact, I think he found her quite charming."

"Yeah, charming in a scary, I'm-putting-a-curse-on-you way," Dani added dryly.

"Hey, all she did was hit his car, and then curse him. Now why wouldn't the man find her charming?" Travis teased.

"She didn't hit his car," Dani said as the elevator doors opened. "She nudged it."

"Nudged it? She totaled the back end of his car and then said it was his fault," Travis pointed out.

Obviously knowing she'd lost this fight, Dani sighed loudly. "Okay, maybe Freda should have handled the situation a little differently."

"A lot differently," he clarified.

"But if she hadn't, then he wouldn't remember her, and we definitely need him to remember her."

"Freda is a hard woman to forget," Travis noted, and then he looked at Dani.

Speaking of hard women to forget, Dani was just like her grandmother. Even though their kiss had been short and tame, he'd already played it back in his mind several times. He'd undoubtedly play it back in his mind many more times, too.

Forgetting Dani was going to take some serious work.

As the elevator doors slid open, the thought hit him that it was probably a good thing Dani was moving away. He wasn't the type to get serious, and if one simple kiss could fog his mind this way, what would happen if they did more than kiss?

Nothing good, that's for sure.

DR. ANDREW KNIGHTLY was a huge man with graying hair who Dani estimated to be in his early fifties. He certainly didn't fit the stereotype of a college professor. There was nothing stuffy or reserved about him. In fact, he was built more like a professional wrestler than an academic.

And when he enthusiastically shook Dani's hand, it was all she could do not to wince.

"Good to meet you." He had a wide smile on his round face and looked completely sincere.

"I'm happy to meet you, too," Dani said, then internally breathed a sigh of relief when he released her poor hand and turned his attention to Travis. She felt as if she should warn Travis about the ferocity of the handshake he was about to experience, but there was no polite way to do it.

Thankfully, Travis seemed to do better than she had. He didn't seem the least uncomfortable as Andrew violently shook his hand.

"I can't believe someone is suing your sweet grandmother," Andrew said once he released Travis's hand. "Even though it was years ago, I still remember how nice and friendly she was."

Dani shot a quick glance at Travis, who seemed as baffled as she was. "I'm surprised to hear you say that since she smashed your car."

Andrew laughed loudly. "Yeah, I know. It seems kind of strange considering that after she plowed into my car, she read me the riot act. But I've always considered myself a good judge of character, and your grandmother is a sweet person at heart."

Well, he was right about that. Her grandmother was a sweet person on the inside. It was the outside that people often misunderstood.

"She told you that love would perpetually confuse you," Dani said, mentally crossing her fingers that this man would be the witness they needed. "Do you feel that her words had any effect on your life?"

Rather than simply blurting out an answer, Dani watched as Andrew seriously considered her question. Finally, he shook his head.

"I've been very fortunate in my life. I fell in love in graduate school. My wife and I have been married for fifteen years and have two great children. I've had a lot of love in my life, but I can't say the emotion has confused me. If anything, I knew the second I met my then-future wife that she was the woman for me." He smiled, obviously enjoying the memory. "She says it was the same for her. One look and we were in love."

Dani really liked his story, and not just because it obviously would help their case. She liked believing that it was possible to meet someone and, pow, know instinctively that they were the right person for you.

She glanced at Travis, wondering what he thought of the story and half-expected him to have a cynical expression on his face. But instead, he was smiling.

"You're a lucky man," Travis told the professor. "And we're lucky, too, because that story is exactly what we need to help Freda."

"Good. I'm glad I can help." He pushed open the door behind him. "Let me show you a picture of my wife and our sons."

Dani happily followed him into the small room, which turned out to be sort of a laboratory. She glanced around, noting rows of cages that lined the counters.

"Is this your lab?" she asked.

Andrew walked over to a desk in the corner and picked up a small picture frame. "Yes. I do behavioral research with animals, mostly mice."

Dani leaned down and looked into one of the cages. A pair of mice were cuddled around each other and sound asleep. "What kind of behavior do you study?"

"Bonding." Andrew handed her the picture.

Dani looked at the happy family. Yes, indeed, this was going to help their case. It was obvious Andrew Knightly and his family all cared deeply about each other.

Perfect.

From across the room, Travis asked, "What exactly do you mean by bonding? Like children bonding to a parent?"

Dani glanced over at him. He was studying a chart on the wall.

"In a way. Certainly, that's the traditional meaning of bonding, but I'm looking into how bonding impacts the mating ritual of mice," Andrew said.

In the back of Dani's mind, a wary feeling started to grow. She tried to push it away, but it kept getting stronger.

"In what way?" she finally asked, now certain she wasn't going to like the answer.

"I know it seems odd, but I'm convinced mice mate for reasons more complicated than mere instinct. I think they form bonds with each other, and that these bonds are based on more than mere proximity during mating periods."

Dani sat on the backless, wooden stool behind her. "What do you think these bonds are?"

"Love, and that's the part that perpetually confuses me," Andrew said with a smile. But as soon as he said the words, silence fell on the room and his smile faded.

"Oh, you don't seriously think that Freda's curse had anything to do with the fact that I'm baffled by the bonding that takes place between mice, do you?" Andrew frowned. "Of course, I do often compare this bonding to the act of humans falling in love, but her curse didn't have a thing to do with it."

Travis moved back to stand next to Dani. He patted her shoulder as he said to Dr. Knightly, "I have to admit, I never thought of mice as falling in love. I thought they just...combined when appropriate."

Andrew nodded. "Most people think that, but I feel there's more at work than simple instinct. I believe that mice form a bond and this bond is similar to what we humans call love."

Dani glanced at the mice in the cages. "So have you been able to prove your theory?"

"Not really. Over the years, my theories have proven hard to show. But I live in hope that soon I'll find a way to prove what I'm sure is fact," he said.

As he wandered over to the big group of cages near the window, Dani glanced up at Travis. He seemed as sad as she felt.

"Love has constantly confused him," she said softly.

"I don't think it's the same thing," Travis insisted.

Andrew turned to face them. "Absolutely. It's not the same thing at all. I don't think that's what your grandmother had in mind. In fact, I'm sure it isn't. I'm sure she was speaking about human love, which has never baffled me."

Despite his words, he didn't sound any more confident than Dani felt. Carl's attorney could easily use this against them.

Dani rubbed her left temple. "I'm afraid we won't be able to use you after all."

He actually looked disappointed. "That's a shame, but I can see how this would complicate matters. Funny, up until you pointed this out, I never even considered her curse as being true. But if you take what she said verbatim, then I guess it's true that love has baffled me my entire life. It just isn't human love that's the culprit."

"Maybe we can find a way to use you still," Travis offered. "Your family life is a real plus."

"But it's not enough," Dani said, unable to believe that once again, her grandmother's curse had come true. This was insane. Freda didn't possess any magical powers. She had no way of making these rantings come true.

Instead, these were coincidences. Strange little cosmic quirks. Normally, Dani would find this situation amusing. After all, it was funny that everything Freda had said seemed to come true.

But she was running out of time to help her grandmother. She needed to pack and get ready for her move. She didn't have time to keep searching all over the place for someone who hadn't had the curse come true.

Still, whether she had time for this or not, she was going to have to keep looking. Because so far, she hadn't accomplished a blasted thing.

5

"I THINK YOU SHOULD USE THE HAPPY ANGLE," Travis said as they pulled out of the parking lot. "Andrew is happy. Peggy is happy. The curses haven't made their lives miserable. They've made them happy."

He thought his argument made a lot of sense but Dani apparently didn't buy it. She shook her head.

"That won't fly. I can't tell this man that, hey, sure the curse worked, but you should be like everyone else Freda cursed—happy." She did a mock shudder. "It would take Carl's lawyer a month to stop laughing."

Travis stopped at a traffic light and looked over at Dani. He could practically feel the tension coming off her. She was under a lot of stress, and so far, nothing they'd tried had helped alleviate that.

"Okay, so then we keep looking," he said. "Sooner or later, we are going to find someone who can help."

"Probably," she said, but he knew she didn't mean it.

"Definitely. So next up is Sarah Davenport. She's a childhood friend of your grandmother's who came to the United States the same year Freda did. They were friends for many, many years. When I spoke to Sarah, she said Freda cursed her one time when they were arguing over a boy. The curse was that love would amaze her. Although Sarah maintains she does find love an amazing emotion, she said that absolutely nothing about the curse has come true in her life. I think she may be perfect for the case."

The light changed, so Travis headed them south toward the small town where Sarah lived. Next to him, Dani was silent, apparently thinking about what he'd just said. He mentally crossed his fingers that Sarah was as good as she sounded, and hey, wasn't it about time they got some good luck? Cursing someone that love would constantly amaze them was like saying the sky was usually blue.

This one should be a slam-dunk.

"I guess it won't hurt to talk to her," Dani finally said. "I'm just feeling so defeated with all these setbacks."

"Yeah, well the curses are kind of general, so in a way, it's how we're interpreting them that's making it look like they came true."

The look she shot him was priceless. "You can't be serious. Anyone is going to interpret Peggy's curse the way we did. The woman has *seven* children. If that's not love in excess, I don't know what is."

"Okay, sure, maybe in her case," he relented. "But in Andrew's case, you can make a strong argument that studying the mating habits of mice is hardly the same thing as being baffled and confused by love.

And I'm certain when Freda cursed him, the last thing she was thinking about was him being baffled by mice."

He had a good point and he could tell she knew it. She leaned her head back against the headrest and sighed.

"You're right. I'm sure Nana wasn't thinking about mice when she cursed Andrew," Dani said. "And if worse comes to worse, I suppose I can use him. If they bring up the mice thing, I can always argue that Freda hates mice and would never have anything to do with them."

"Exactly." Travis studied her. She looked a little happier now.

"So if we end up absolutely stuck, I guess we'll use Andrew." Dani sat up straight in her seat.

"That's the spirit." He exited the interstate and then turned into the parking lot of a restaurant. Time for food. But before they got out of the car, he reached over and patted her leg. "Things will work out."

He'd intended the pat to be one of comfort. Bad mistake. Instead of a friendly gesture, the second his hand touched her bare skin, desire shot through him like a charge of electricity.

He found his willful hand lingering, and the pat he'd intended quickly turned into a caress. Damn hand. It should know better.

But it didn't, so Travis kept expecting Dani to grab his hand and move it while she simultaneously gave him a lecture on how they'd agreed to be friends only.

Unfortunately, she didn't do either of those things. Instead, she covered his hand with her own.

"We need to stop doing things like this," she said, her voice soft and seductive.

Travis nodded and continued to caress her leg. "Absolutely."

"It's not smart."

"Not a bit." He slid his hand higher on her leg.

"So we'll stop," she said, but since her voice was raspy with desire, he knew she didn't mean a word she'd said.

He felt like a high-school kid all over again, as if he were trying to get away with something. As if he were trying to impress the girl with his moves.

Yeah, but there was nothing smooth or cool about this situation. And he was way too old for games, especially with someone like Dani.

Once again he reminded himself that she was a friend. A client. The last woman he should be fooling around with in his car.

That did it. Reluctantly, he removed his hand.

"You know, I haven't a clue what's going on between us," he admitted. "But I haven't given up on the theory that I've lost my mind."

"Then I've lost mine, too," she said, her gaze holding his. "Is insanity contagious?"

He sighed. "I don't know. I'm beginning to think so. In high school, there was never anything between us. Zip. Nothing." He glanced at the restaurant door and then back at her. "Unless I missed something."

She shook her head. "No. I know all the girls were wild about you, but honestly, Travis, to me you were just a friend."

"So where's all this attraction coming from now?"

"Haven't a clue," she admitted.

"Well, if you don't know and I don't know, who does?"

She shrugged. "Beats me."

"We certainly can't ask Dr. Knightly because we already know love and attraction baffle him."

His nonsense had the expected result. She laughed, breaking the weird sexual tension in the car.

"True," she finally managed to say. "I have a suggestion. I say we ignore the annoying attraction. I'm sure after a while it will go away."

"Think we can do it?" He honestly didn't think it would work. Normally, he felt in complete control when it came to relationships. He kept them light. He kept them simple. If they started to be complicated, he pulled the plug.

But this attraction he felt for Dani was different. It went way beyond the typical isn't-she-hot attraction. Sure, Dani was cute. But she was also fun and funny and smart. He really admired and respected her.

And *that* made him nervous as hell.

"I think we can. Want to give it a try?" she asked.

"I guess. Plus, what do we have to lose?"

LIFE REALLY had it in for her, Dani decided as she finished filling out the paperwork for a room at the

Sleepy Inn, a small bed and breakfast on the out-
skirts of town. She and Travis had just agreed to ignore the attraction between them when Sarah called
and asked to postpone their meeting until the morning. Since it was too far to drive back home now,
they'd been left with no choice but to find a place to
stay in town.

Although they would have preferred a modern
hotel, there was a local football game tonight that
had filled up all the cheaper places. In fact, the only
reason they'd been able to get a room at the Sleepy
Inn was because of a last-minute cancellation.

"People don't miss the chance to see the Tigers
play the Cougars," the owner of the Sleepy Inn, Louise Reardon, said as she led them up the winding
stairs to their rooms. "This is a rivalry that goes back
decades. I'm sure you'll want to go to the game even
if you're not from around here. It's the event of the
year. Those boys really go at it."

"Really," Dani said, only partially listening. Her
attention was focused on the man following her. Although she and Travis had agreed to ignore the attraction between them, an overnight stay at a hotel
wouldn't make things any easier.

"Oh, yes." Louise laughed, her white curls bob-
bing. "Personally, I don't care who wins because
it's all green money to me. The inn is packed on
Tiger-Cougar weekend. Anyhoo, you really should
go to the game. Neither team is that good, but
they're about equally bad, so it's interesting. And

the crowd goes crazy. That in itself is the best reason to go."

"I'm not sure we can make it," Dani said.

She glanced at Travis, who shrugged. She felt bad for him. He was carrying a lot. First, he had the bag of things she'd bought at a local store when they'd realized they were going to have to spend the night here. Then he had a duffel bag with his spare clothes that he thankfully carried in his car at all times. When Dani had teased him about it, he'd explained that as a PI, he never knew what was going to happen and liked to be prepared.

In addition to their things, he also had two boxes Louise had asked him to bring upstairs. Dani had offered several times to help and had tried in vain to grab her things before he did, but in typical macho male fashion, he'd picked up everything and was now pretending it wasn't killing him carrying it all up the narrow, winding steps.

Poor baby.

"If you need tickets, just stop by the front desk later and I'll give you a couple," Louise prattled on, apparently unconcerned that they might be damaging Travis's back forever.

"We'll think about it," Dani said, sending another concerned look over her shoulder at Travis. She had to admit, he didn't seem to be struggling even though she knew those boxes Louise had given him weighed a ton. He must work out.

Of course, that would explain the muscles she'd

felt the night he'd kissed her. As they'd kissed, she'd placed her left hand on his arm and had definitely been impressed by the muscles she'd felt. In fact, those biceps had been almost as impressive as the kiss. And thinking back on it, the kiss had been—

"Anything I can help you with?" Travis asked, coming up to stand close to her. He must have had some inkling as to what she was thinking about, because he had a fairly cocky look on his face.

Dani blinked and looked around. Drat. Apparently she was indeed impressed by his biceps since she'd stopped in her tracks while she'd considered them.

She turned and saw Louise had reached the top of the stairs and was looking at her with concern.

"Are you having a mini-stroke?" Louise asked her. Before Dani could answer, the older woman continued, "My cousin, Eugenia, had a mini-stroke once. We went for a walk, and I was talking about this thing on my right foot that I thought might be a bunion. See, I had a friend whose cousin was married to a man who used to live next door to a fellow whose aunt knew a man who had a bunion that grew so big, it eventually killed him." She made a tsking noise. "So sad. I don't want to go that way."

Dani opened her mouth to say that story didn't sound very plausible to her, when Louise started talking again.

"So naturally, I was concerned that *I* might have a bunion. Anyhoo, after about twenty minutes, Eugenia froze like a stream during January. She just stopped walking and talking and kind of stared off into space like she was dreaming. Kinda the way you did just now, Dani. I kept talking to her for the longest time before I realized something was wrong. Finally, she looked at me and said she thought she'd had a mini-stroke and that she needed quiet for a while." Louise tipped her head and studied Dani. "Do you think you might have had a mini-stroke?"

A muffled laugh floated over Dani's shoulders. She bit back the smile that was threatening to form on her face and told Louise in the most serious voice she could manage, "No. I'm fine. I was...thinking about something."

She knew Travis knew exactly what that something she'd been thinking about was, but she refused to look at him. Instead, she finished climbing the stairs and then walked next to Louise, her gaze remaining fixed in front of her.

"You two are lucky you're not having to share a room," Louise said. "We normally don't get couples wanting separate rooms. I know you said you're just friends, but usually when people are friends, it means that they still like to..." She waved both hands in the air and then winked with great exaggeration at Dani. "Get ex-er-cise."

Dani stopped and stared at the woman. "Um..."

Louise kept on walking down the hallway so Dani hurried to catch up. "See, I saw a talk show once that said it used to be years ago that you waited until you were married to, you know, exercise, and then you only exercised with the person you'd married."

She glanced at Dani, obviously expecting some sort of response, but the best Dani could manage was "hmmm."

Fortunately, that seemed to be enough for Louise, because she just kept talking. "Then in the sixties and seventies, people exercised with all sorts of other people, but we all know where that ended up."

Again she stopped and looked at Dani. This time, Dani was ready for her. She managed to say, "Interesting," which wasn't much, but it was better than "hmmm."

Louise started walking once more. "Now they say that when young people aren't ready to settle down, they find a friend they really like, someone special, and they *exercise* with that person until they find the person they want to marry and spend their lives with. They call it friends with benefits. Isn't that sweet?"

This time when Louise looked at Dani for a response, she couldn't think of a single thing to say. Her mind was a complete blank. Instead, she just stared at the older woman. Louise looked as though she should be on the cover of a package of old-fashioned chocolate-chip cookies instead of discussing sex.

Louise smiled a dreamy sort of smile. "Anyhoo, that's what Frank and I decided to do. After my Henry died eight years ago, I figured I'd given up exercise. But then I saw this show and realized that Frank and I are great friends. Sure, we'll never get married or anything, but we like each other, so why not exercise together?"

Dani exerted every drop of willpower she had to keep her mouth from falling open. Talk about being given *way* too much information. Dani could only hope Louise was done now because she wasn't sure how much more she could take.

"Plus, since Frank works here, it's convenient. We both understand what we're doing, so no one gets hurt." Louise leaned toward Dani. "I mean, don't get me wrong—we take all the precautions you're supposed to take these days. But this way, it's very efficient." She smiled at Dani. "Do you know what I mean?"

Sadly, Dani understood all too well what the older woman meant. She couldn't remember ever having a more awkward conversation with someone she didn't know in the slightest. Despite herself, Dani glanced at Travis, who looked as though he was about to burst into laughter. When he caught Dani's gaze, he grinned his sexy grin and she knew she was in big trouble.

"Um, is my room around here somewhere?" Dani asked, forcing herself to look away from Travis and hoping to change the topic of conversation.

"Right here," Louise said, stopping in front of a white door and unlocking it. "I think you're going to really like this. I decorated it myself after watching one of those shows on TV where they take an ugly room and make it beautiful."

Dani braced herself for what might be inside, and then slowly followed the other woman. But the second she walked in, Dani fell in love with the room. Louise had used delicate flowered paper on the walls, and then coordinated the duvet and drapes to match. In the corner by the fireplace was a large chair that begged to be sat in, and over by the window was a window seat with countless throw pillows.

The overall effect was one of elegance mixed with comfort.

"This place is wonderful," Dani said, setting her purse on the small antique table next to the bed. "You did a great job."

On the hope chest at the end of the bed, Travis set the bag with the essentials she'd bought. He glanced around the room, and Dani barely managed not to tease him about his horrified expression.

Unable to resist, she asked sweetly, "So what do you think of my room, Travis?"

"Um, well," he said as he continued to survey the room. "It's definitely...flowery."

Louise laughed. "Men always react like we've dipped them in tar when they see this room, but the women love it. And we find that by the next morning, the men have stopped noticing what the room looks like. They usually find other things to look at."

This time, Louise did her exaggerated wink at Travis, which only made him look even more horrified.

"Louise, could you show us Travis's room?" Dani asked, trying to rescue him.

Louise headed out the door, and the look Travis shot her made Dani roll her eyes. Yes, Louise was something else.

Once they were all in the hall again, Louise had Travis put the two big boxes in a storage closet. Then she opened a door right next to Dani's room.

As the door swung open, Dani expected more flowers, but there wasn't a single rose or tulip in sight. Rather than flowers and fritz, his room was clean lines and dark woods. The bed was as impressive as the one in her room, but instead of flowers, it was covered in a thick, burgundy spread. The furniture was mahogany and huge, made for comfort and relaxation.

"Now this is a man's room." Dani walked inside and said in a deep voice, "Heck, even I feel macho in this room."

Travis chuckled and set his duffel bag on the dresser. "Okay, I'll admit this room is nice. And it doesn't creep me out like your room does."

"Hey, my room isn't creepy. It's refined and genteel."

"It's what most women expect when they come to a bed and breakfast," Louise said. "They expect antiques and frills."

"And they get it in that room. It's definitely feminine," he said, heading across the room and opening a set of French doors that led to a balcony. "Man, that's what I call a view."

Dani came over to join him on the small wooden balcony. Since both rooms were at the back of the inn, they faced a broad meadow that had a stream running through it. The sun was setting and the view was still spectacular. Trees swayed in the early evening air and Dani felt surrounded by peace and serenity.

"Okay, now I'm even more in love," Dani said.

"It is pretty, isn't it?" Louise had a grin on her face as she motioned to the door by the highboy. "Anyhoo, one more thing I want to point out. Just in case you change you mind about…you know, *ex-er-cise*, that door connects your two rooms." With another grin, she added, "Have fun."

She wiggled her fingers in what Dani assumed was a wave, then walked out, shutting the door behind her. Once the older woman was gone, Dani looked at Travis.

With a chuckle, he said, "Do you get the feeling she wants us to get some *exercise* tonight?"

Dani laughed, glad Travis had joked about it. "I couldn't believe it when she started suggesting we use each other as *exercise* partners. She doesn't even know us."

Travis nodded, but made no comment. Despite that nod, the thoughtful look on his face made Dani wonder if he might be thinking about what Louise had suggested.

But it was ridiculous. She was leaving town in a few days. This was the wrong time to get involved. Okay, so Louise hadn't been suggesting they get involved. In fact, quite the contrary. But now was the wrong time to *exercise*, also.

Wasn't it?

Glancing back at Travis, she had to admit, the idea was tantalizing. Louise had made some good points. As long as both parties understood what was happening, no one got hurt.

But she didn't want to think about this right now, especially with Travis standing so close and looking so handsome. Instead, she sank into one of the white wooden lounge chairs on the balcony and closed her eyes.

"I'm just going to stay here for a while absorbing the quiet."

"Nope. First you've got to feed me," Travis said.

"Feed you?" She opened her eyes and looked up at him. "You're all grown up. You can feed yourself."

He walked over to stand next to her, and just that was enough for Dani's IQ to start dropping. When had being close to Travis become this distracting? At some point in the last couple of days, her body had definitely taken on a mind of its own. She found herself leaning even closer to him and resenting the few inches that separated them.

So much for being able to resist the attraction between them.

"What fun would eating alone be? I haven't seen my old high-school friend, Dani Karlinski, for years. I want to spend some time with her," Travis said.

As reasonable as his explanation sounded, she

hadn't forgotten what had happened the last time they'd had dinner together, and she felt he needed to be reminded.

"Eating out with an old friend is what caused the kiss to happen last time," she pointed out.

Travis didn't say a word for several seconds. Instead, he met her gaze. She could clearly see the conflict he was feeling. He liked her as a friend, enjoyed spending time with her—and wanted her.

She knew he could see the same expression on her face. Dani couldn't remember a time she'd ever been this confused about a man. They could say they'd ignore this attraction between them all they wanted to, but it was turning out to be impossible. Louise's suggestion about being friends with benefits was getting more appealing by the second.

Finally, Travis said, "Guess we'll just have to see where life leads us."

"Guess so," she said. "In the meantime, why don't we see if this inn has a dining room?"

"Good plan." Travis held out his hand, and without thinking, Dani took it. Sparks of attraction danced across her fingers as his warm skin brushed hers.

Oh, yes. Being friends with benefits was definitely becoming appealing.

"WHICH TEAM should we root for?" Travis asked as he scanned the field. They'd ended up at the high-school football game because there was really no place else to go. The dining room at the inn was closed, as were most of the restaurants in town. Seemed like every local business had a sign in the window that said they'd gone to the game.

Left with limited options, Travis and Dani had gone to the game, too. If they wanted food, this was the only place to get it. So far, they'd both had hot dogs and sodas. Not exactly a healthy dinner, but at least it had been food.

"Cougars or Tigers?" he asked again.

At that moment, some of the people near them hollered, "Go Cougars!"

Dani nodded toward the crowd. Everyone was decorated in Cougar gear and chanting for the home team.

"Cougars, of course," she said, with a laugh.

Travis grinned. "Seems like the best idea, especially if we want to get out of here alive."

As it turned out, he hadn't been kidding when he'd said it would be a wise choice. The people around here took their football seriously, and the Cougar-Tiger rivalry obviously ran deep. From the comments he overheard, Travis took it that the Cougars felt the Tigers often cheated. But as he stood in line for refills on the sodas, he overheard several Tiger fans say the exact same thing about the Cougars.

Ah, high-school football. He'd forgotten how intense it could be. He'd played on the football team his last three years in high school. Tonight brought back some great memories. Memories of success on the field. And memories of some successes off the field. Nothing like being a high school quarterback to make the cheerleaders notice you.

"The Cougars just scored again," Dani said, coming over to stand next to him in line. "Bet this is like old times for you. Football. *Scoring*."

Travis chuckled but he wasn't about to admit to her that he'd been thinking along the same lines. "I do miss playing football. It was fun."

"Yeah, football. I'm sure that's all you miss," she said with a devilish grin.

He grinned back at her. "I miss it because I don't still play football."

Dani laughed and bumped his arm. "I see your point."

The line moved forward, so they shifted with the rest of the people. "Why didn't you wait in the seats? I can get the sodas without help."

Dani was studying the menu. "I'm hungry."

"How? You just demolished a foot-long hot dog and a huge soda."

"Hey, it's been a long time since I've been at a game, so I need to eat all of my favorites while I'm here. I don't want to miss out on any experiences."

At her last comment, he turned and looked at her. Did she mean that the way it sounded or was she really just talking about concession-stand food?

He couldn't tell from her expression, not even when she turned her head and met his gaze. Dani had the most amazing eyes, but they held all of her secrets close. He could never tell what she was thinking.

But as far as he was concerned, there was no point pretending anymore. Louise had made a good point. Being friends with benefits was fine as long as no one got hurt.

"I'm all for not missing experiences," he said as desire simmered through his veins. He certainly couldn't be clearer than that. Now he just had to see what Dani thought of the idea.

"Not missing experiences is a good thing, I've decided," she said. Then with a sexy smile that made his heart slam in his chest, she added, "Just like exercise is a good thing. I've decided that *ex-er-cise* would be a very good thing."

Man, he hadn't expected her to say that. When they'd talked about this possibility before, they'd both agreed they should avoid getting involved.

He knew she was waiting for his reaction, so he leaned down and lightly brushed her lips with his own.

"Exercise seems like an excellent idea," he said. Then he took her hand. "Want to head back to the inn?"

She threaded her fingers through his. "Definitely. We can find out tomorrow who won the game."

"As far as I'm concerned, we did," he said. Then they headed to the car.

6

Now that they'd made the decision, Dani could hardly wait to get back to the b&b. She couldn't remember ever wanting a man the way she wanted Travis. Sure, he was handsome and sexy as sin, but the desire she felt for him went way beyond the physical. He was smart and kind and fun, and she knew he would be a considerate and inventive lover.

"Not getting cold feet, are you?" he asked when they were almost there.

"No. You?"

He flashed her a grin. "Not hardly."

She liked that he felt the same frantic level of desire that she felt, and she found herself wishing he'd drive faster. When they got stopped by a red light, she groaned.

"I know for a fact it didn't take this long to drive *from* the inn to the stadium. Why is it taking so long to drive back?" she asked, not really expecting an answer.

"I guess right now wouldn't be the best time to point out that good things come to those who wait," he told her, reaching over and taking one of her hands in his.

"That's sweet, Travis, but no offense, what bunk."

He chuckled. "Okay, then is it any consolation to know I'm just as anxious as you are?"

Actually, it was, and she smiled. "Yes. I want to know you're suffering the same way I am."

"Ah. I see. Well, I am."

She nodded, and then the second the light turned green, said, "Let's go."

The rest of the way to the inn, Dani found herself counting the seconds. Finally, Travis pulled in to the parking lot and found a space. Dani shoved open her door and met him in front of the car. When he took her hand again in his, she couldn't help squeezing his fingers.

Unable to go any longer without a little something to tide her over, she leaned up and kissed him.

"This is going to be great," she said when the kiss ended.

Travis kissed her again. "Oh, yeah."

Tugging on his hand, Dani led the way inside and up the stairs. When they reached their rooms, she didn't hesitate. She headed to his.

"I don't want you getting distracted by the flowers in my room," she told him.

"I won't be looking at the walls," he pointed out as he unlocked the door to his room and hustled them inside.

Once there, he turned to face her. She started to

move closer, but before she could take a step, he held up one hand.

"Last chance to change your mind," he said.

Dani laughed. He was so sweet. "Not going to happen," she assured him.

He grinned and that grin was enough to snap what little control she had. She practically jumped on Travis, and with a laugh, he caught her and they staggered to the bed. He dropped her onto the soft mattress and then sat next to her.

"I can tell this is going to be a wild night," he joked.

She laughed. "I think you're right."

Then, without hesitation or awkwardness, she pulled her T-shirt over her head.

Travis did the same thing. "Your turn," he told her.

The great thing about being with a man you were friends with is that you could make the experience fun, Dani decided. She'd known Travis for years, had shared many experiences with him, and had had a great time with him.

Sex was going to be one more experience for them to share together. She knew it would be better than anything she'd experienced before because they cared and liked each other.

She was about to remove her bra when he leaned over and kissed her softly. Unexpectedly, his kiss was gentle, but it still made her body feel alive. She curled into his kiss, wrapping her arms around his waist, pressing her breasts to his chest.

Travis tipped his head and deepened the kiss,

shifting her so her body aligned with his. When she pressed against him, she could feel how much he wanted her.

Oh, my.

With a little squeak of excitement, she let her hands dance across his bare chest, caressing his warm skin, feeling the strong muscles shift beneath her touch. She felt on fire for him, as if she couldn't get enough.

Travis seemed to share her sentiment, because his kiss turned more passionate, more possessive. His tongue explored her mouth, gliding against her own.

As they kissed, Travis reached behind her and undid her bra. Dani helped him take it off, wanting to feel his touch on her breasts.

"You're so beautiful," he murmured. "And so special."

Since he was still kissing her with his eyes closed, he hadn't even looked at her yet. Knowing that he meant she was beautiful in a way that had nothing to do with her looks made her feel warm and cherished.

She broke off the kiss and when he opened his eyes and looked at her, she said, "You're beautiful, too, Travis. And very special to me."

He smiled slowly, and that sexy smile told her of things to come. She felt need pool inside her, and then all tender thoughts were quickly replaced by hot, searing, desirous ones as Travis leaned over and drew one of her taut nipples into his mouth and suckled.

Dani's breath caught in her throat as he shifted his

attention from one breast to another, lavishing kisses and caresses on both.

When the tension inside her had built to a fever pitch, she sat up and fumbled with the button on his jeans.

"In a hurry?" he asked, flashing her yet another of those sexy smiles.

She didn't even try to pretend. "Yes."

Rather than tease her about her impatience, Travis quickly pulled off his jeans and boxers, then helped her shed the rest of her own clothes.

When he was naked, Dani couldn't help admiring how gorgeous he was. Unable to refrain, she skimmed her hands down his toned body, torturing him as he'd tortured her with a combination of fleeting touches and lingering caresses.

"Wow," she said as she caressed his length.

Travis laughed. "Yeah, sure, I'm pin-up material."

She encircled him, running her hand up and down his shaft. "Definitely."

Travis kissed her again, his own hands as busy as hers were. Dani's heart slammed in her chest with excitement when he finally slipped one large hand between her thighs and caressed her in a slow, delightful rhythm.

"Travis," she murmured against his lips as he drove her crazy with his talented fingers. As the pressure inside her built, she arched off the bed, searching for release that was so close, and yet just out of her grasp.

"Travis," she said again, this time with more urgency as he increased the rhythm, until finally, blissfully, sweet release found her.

For several long seconds afterward, she struggled to breathe normally again. Eventually, she turned her head to look at him. "I know I keep saying this, but wow."

He smiled. "Glad you liked it. Want to try some other things?"

"Definitely," she said.

Despite her protests, he started to move away. He shot her a smoldering look. "I'm not leaving. Just getting condoms."

When he opened his duffel bag and took out a small drug store bag, she shot him a knowing look.

"You were counting on this happening, weren't you?" she teased.

"We'd shared one hell of a kiss," he told her. "I like to be prepared."

Personally, she was thrilled about his preparations. When he returned to the bed, she plucked a condom from the box and opened it.

"Want me to help you with that?" he offered.

She smiled at him, enjoying herself immensely, and shook her head. "No. I think I can handle things fine on my own."

And she did, until the amount of handling she did caused Travis to groan with pleasure. When she completed her task, she climbed on top of him before he could protest—although she was pretty sure he wouldn't have protested. He seemed more than happy with her idea.

Dani took him slowly inside her body, enjoying the sensation of completeness. Once she was settled, she set a steady, pounding pace guaranteed to drive them both insane.

Finally, with a moan that sounded pretty close to a growl, Travis rolled them both over so she was beneath him. He held her gaze as he drove into her time and again with a frenzy she matched.

With one final thrust, he called out her name and they both shattered, their climaxes wild and wonderful and beyond anything Dani had ever imagined, let alone experienced.

Later, as he held her in his arms, she realized one indisputable fact—whatever else happened to her in life, she would never forget this night with Travis. No other person had ever understood her the way he did, and she knew that what they'd shared was so much more than sex. She felt truly content, a feeling she couldn't remember ever experiencing before.

A CLANKING NOISE woke Travis with a start. He opened his eyes, and then, in the faint light coming in through the open room door, he saw that Dani was setting a tray on the desk across the room.

"What are you doing?" he asked, only half awake. He glanced at the clock by his bed. It was a little after one in the morning.

"Sorry. I didn't mean to wake you. I was hungry

so I went looking for food," she said, waving one hand at the tray. "When I reached the kitchen, Louise was still up. The second I said I wanted something to eat, she gave me a ton of stuff." Dani grinned. "Want some?"

Now that he was awake and thought about it, he was hungry, too. "Sure."

He turned on the light next to the bed, blinking at the brightness. When he saw what Dani was wearing, he couldn't help laughing. Although she looked adorable, she had on her jeans with his T-shirt.

"Did she comment on your outfit?" he asked, pulling on his boxers, and then shutting the door to the room. He went to stand next to her, adding, "I bet Louise had a field day with that."

Dani glanced at her outfit and smiled. "Surprisingly, she didn't say a word. But I think that's why I ended up with so much food. I think she knew we'd decided she had the right idea about friends with benefits. Why else would she give me so much?"

He studied the tray. Louise had loaded it with sandwiches, chips, sodas and brownies, more than enough for two.

"She must have known," he agreed.

"Either way, I think my search for food was a success," she said, snagging a chip off one of the plates. "I was worried I would come back empty-handed."

Travis pulled out a chair for Dani, and after she sat, he took the chair across from her.

"You did an excellent job," he said, waiting until

she had selected a sandwich before choosing one of his own. "I don't think a professional food scavenger could have done better."

Dani laughed. "Good to know I have another career option."

"Definitely." He smiled at her, enjoying the look of happiness on her face.

When she took a bite of her sandwich, she made a blissful, sexy sound. "It absolutely doesn't get better than this."

As he ate his sandwich, he had to agree. This was darn good. Not only the food, but also the company. The past few hours had been amazing, beyond his expectations, which had been pretty high.

He and Dani had had sex, not just once, but three times. Three times with each time becoming more wild and frantic and earth-shattering than the time before. Sure, he'd had great sex before, but this had been different. Being with Dani had been different. Everything about it had been more intense. Every touch and look they'd shared had seemed to bring them even closer together. He knew he should be rattled by what had happened, but he wasn't. Being with Dani felt right, and nothing on this planet could stop him from spending as much time as possible with her.

When she started to reach for a soda, Travis got it for her. She tipped her head and studied him, a small smile lurking around her lips.

"You have such wonderful manners," she said, almost to herself rather than to him. "I remember you always had wonderful manners."

Travis chuckled. "Hey, that's what all guys want to hear after making love to a woman—that they have great manners."

She laughed, and nudged him under the table with her knee. "That wasn't what I was talking about. You know I thought you were sensational in bed."

Despite himself, he grinned. "Yeah, you, too."

Dani continued to study him. Then she asked, "Did your father teach you manners?"

Realizing she really did want to talk about this, Travis took a sip of his soda, then explained, "My dad wasn't exactly what you would call an involved parent. But since my mother took off when Max and I were little and we never heard from her again, he was all we had. He wasn't mean to us. He just ignored us. So for many years, we kind of ran wild."

"Did you get into a lot of trouble?"

He shook his head. "Nope. We were never that bad. Just rough around the edges. Until we were stationed in Japan."

When he paused, Dani smiled. "What happened?"

"The woman who lived next door to us grabbed Max and me one day and chewed us out for being what she called 'Wild-West outlaws' and having no manners. She told us we were guests in Japan and that we were a poor reflection on our country and that we'd never amount to anything."

When Dani gave him a soft look that told him she

felt sorry for him, he laughed. "No, it wasn't a mean thing. She was right. We were out of control. By telling us we'd never be anything, she got our attention. And then she did something that made all the difference. She dared us."

Dani frowned. "Dared you?"

"She dared us to learn how to behave like gentlemen. She said if we could prove we'd learned how to behave, she'd cook us four homemade dinners. If we failed, then we had to clean her house once a week for a month."

Dani laughed. "How old were you two?"

"I was eight. Max was ten. And a dare is a sacred thing, so naturally we accepted."

With a smirk on her face, Dani said, "Of course. Did you win?"

He pretended to be insulted. "Of course we won. Although it wasn't easy since we knew nothing about manners. We ended up finding a book at the base library on manners that had been written a couple of decades earlier, so we picked up a few habits that were out of style. But we did learn the basics, and we really enjoyed those homemade meals."

"What a great story. And I'm so happy to hear you didn't have to clean that woman's house after all."

"Oh, sure we did," Travis admitted. "The book said that polite people do nice things for other people. Naturally, Max and I took that to mean that we should clean her house, so we did."

She gave him a soft, sweet look and said, "Okay,

I didn't think it was possible to like you any more than I already do, but you've proven me wrong."

The way she was looking at him made Travis more than a little nervous, so he admitted, "Just remember, there are a lot of stories I could tell you that wouldn't make you think I'm a nice guy."

But instead of discouraging her, Dani simply shook her head. "I doubt it. You're a good person, Travis Walker."

Feeling unsettled and embarrassed by this conversation, he cleared his throat and asked, "So what about you? Where did you learn your manners?"

"I'm pretty sure I was taught in the womb," she said, rolling her eyes. "You've met my mother. She wouldn't stand for a child being rude, or making noise for that matter."

Yeah, Dani's mother definitely struck him as the children-should-be-seen-but-not-heard type.

"Must have been tough," he said.

"It was difficult." She moved the food around on her plate. "That's why I love Freda so much. When she moved into our house, she brought life and energy and fun. Despite all her efforts, my mother has never been able to subdue her. Freda does what Freda wants to do, and as a little girl, I thought she was magical."

"Freda is her own woman," he said.

She took a bite of one of the brownies, then added, "I know, and that's why I still think my grandmother is one of the most unique people I've ever met. I admire her a lot. She lives life on her own terms, which very few people do. I guess in a way, I still think she's magical."

Travis smiled and pointed out, "And we're finding out that may be true in more ways than just one."

With a nod, Dani said, "True. I really am starting to think maybe she's right, maybe there's something to these curses after all. Oh, right, they're romantic suggestions, not curses. Whatever they are, they shouldn't work, but they seem to."

Travis studied Dani, he was going to miss her after she moved. He liked listening to her, liked talking to her. She was so unique, so different from other women he knew

"I'm sorry things aren't working out for the case," he admitted.

She shrugged. "I can't think about that right now. We'll just have to see how tomorrow goes." She stood and asked, "Want to go back to bed?"

"Are you tired?" He glanced at the bed and then back at her. Personally, he'd never felt more awake in his life, and sleeping was the last thing on his mind at the moment.

Dani flashed him a sassy smile and pulled his T-shirt off over her head. "I wasn't exactly thinking about sleeping."

At that moment, Travis knew he was going to have to be careful, because if ever there were a woman he could fall for, it would be this one.

7

DANI OPENED her eyes slowly, not wanting the harsh morning light to spoil the magic of last night. It didn't, at least not completely. Travis was still next to her, one of his long arms draped across her waist.

For a selfish moment, Dani kept perfectly still and a silly thought ran through her mind—maybe if she didn't move, the spell would never be broken. That surreal feeling she'd had for the past few hours would never leave. It was a feeling of rightness, a feeling of completeness.

An absolute certainty that something special and unique had happened.

"I can hear you thinking," Travis murmured, and then he leaned forward and kissed her back. "You're thinking way too loudly this morning."

"Ha. Shows what you know. I was not thinking," she teased, turning over to face him.

It wasn't fair. How could he look even sexier when rumpled and sleepy? She knew she didn't look her best first thing in the morning, but Travis did. He should be on a poster selling something. With his broad shoulders, devil's grin, and early-morning stubble, the man was sexy enough to sell flippers to fish.

Amazing.

He cocked one eyebrow. "Even now you're thinking, and no good can come from thinking the morning after a night of rowdy sex."

Dani smiled, enjoying the camaraderie and banter they shared. "Oh, really? You sure about that?"

He skimmed one hand down her body, his talented fingers reawakening her desire. "Absolutely. The only way to approach a morning after is to reconfirm that all the pleasure felt the night before was real and not just an illusion."

She pretended to think about what he'd said. "Hmmm. Is that the *only* way? Seems to me that there would be hundreds of ways to approach the morning after. Maybe we should try some of those other ways first."

Travis leaned forward and nibbled on her chin. "No. There's only one that works. And since there is only one approach, the smart thing to do would be to follow that approach. Then we could verify for ourselves that last night wasn't just the world's most erotic dream. That it was, in fact, real."

Any thought she'd had of discussing this further slipped away when he started kissing his way down her body. His kisses were warm and lingering and determined to arouse.

She might have managed a small protest if he'd stopped after lavishing both breasts with his mouth, but he didn't. Instead, he kept moving until finally he found his destination. And after he'd shifted her thighs and focused his attention, Dani lost the ability to think at all.

TRAVIS SCANNED the room, making sure they hadn't left anything behind, but the place was clean. Not just tidy, but spotlessly clean. Not surprisingly, Dani was a neat person.

At some point after they'd shared a shower that had lasted a long, long time, she must have straightened the bed and picked up every trace that they'd ever been in the room.

The woman needed to relax.

He glanced over at her. She was putting on makeup.

"You cleaned the room," he said.

"I didn't want Louise to think we were slobs."

He chuckled and walked over to stand behind her. He picked up her brush and slowly ran it through her long, dark hair. "More importantly, we don't want her to know we followed her advice and did some exercising last night."

"I think she already figured that out when I went down for snacks." Dani closed her eyes as he continued to brush her hair. "And by the way, what we did last night was more than mere exercise."

"I think it was the Olympics of sex," he said with a laugh. What had started out as fun had quickly turned into something explosive. They'd each been hungry for the other, and no amount of lovemaking seemed to satisfy their appetites.

Frankly, he was surprised he could still walk this morning. But even now, even after hours of making love to Dani, all he could think about was how much he wanted her again. Rationally, he knew that sort of unquenchable desire for her should bother him, but oddly, it didn't.

"I can't believe I'm about to say this, but you want to talk about last night?" he asked, and immediately felt like hitting himself in the head with the brush. How dumb could he be? Here was a beautiful woman who didn't seem compelled to discuss what was happening between them. Why couldn't he just accept that? Normally, he'd give anything for a woman who would simply accept the situation.

But this time with Dani was different. Last night had been different. He might joke, at least a little, about it being the Olympics of sex, but it had been a hell of a lot more than that. There was a connection between them.

Always had been.

He knew it. And he knew she knew it, too.

"I thought we'd agreed beforehand that we were simply following Louise's advice and using each other as friends with benefits," Dani said, opening her eyes and locking her gaze with his in the mirror. "I don't think either one of us wants it to be more complicated than that."

But it was more complicated. Something had happened last night, some bond had been formed. That connection between them had deepened and become meaningful.

They both knew this was more than just exercise. He could see in her eyes that she'd felt what he'd felt. But he could also see in her eyes the need to ignore what had happened. It wasn't easy, especially since he'd never felt anything like this before. But the lady was right.

There was no percentage in hashing this out. Dani was moving to New York soon. Those plans couldn't be changed. He was a partner in Walker Investigations. He'd worked too hard for too many years to blow that away so he could follow Dani to New York. Plus, he owed his brother. He couldn't walk out on Max. For most of their lives, it had been the two of them against the world.

He could never bail on his brother.

So *exercise* was all this could be.

"I hear exercise is good for you," he teased to lighten the mood.

She rewarded him with a sexy smile. "Oh, really?"

He slipped his hands around her waist and fiddled with the buttons of a shirt of his that she was wearing. "Yes. Exercise is very, very good for you."

"I would have thought you'd had enough exercise to last you quite some time," she said, her voice becoming noticeably breathy when he popped a few of the buttons free.

"I'm a firm believer in the theory of the more exercise, the better." He turned her so she faced him, then he leaned down to brush his lips across hers.

As he hoped, Dani readily accepted his invitation. She slipped her arms around his neck and then murmured, "Let's see just how firm a believer you are."

DANI LOOKED at the notes she'd written down about Sarah Davenport and then mentally crossed her fingers. The woman was a dog breeder and had had a dog give birth the previous night. Complications had resulted, so she'd wanted to be there, but this afternoon, she'd said on the phone, she had plenty of time to talk to them.

Even though Dani was hoping for the best, she realized her track record wasn't very good.

"I don't see how Sarah can disappoint us," Travis said as he turned off the main road and headed down the narrow winding path leading to Sarah's house. "The woman is a happily married dog breeder. She runs a family business with her husband, two grown daughters and her granddaughter."

"Nana said that love would amaze her," Dani said, drumming her fingers on her leg, nervous tension coiling inside of her. This was their last shot, the last person Dani had time to visit. It had to work. "I don't even want to consider what that curse could mean."

"I have a good feeling about this one." Travis reached over and patted her hand, stopping her nervous action. She knew the gesture was intended to be comforting, but as always when he touched her, she felt a tingle of awareness. How was it possible to want a man you'd just spent the better part of ten hours making love to? Amazing.

She was glad they were being sensible about their relationship. As Louise had said, as long as you agreed to things up front, there was no reason why a relationship based strictly on friendship and sex couldn't work.

Good grief, if Louise could make such a relationship work, then surely she and Travis could. They were both mature adults who'd been involved in relationships before. They understood priorities and goals and appreciated each other's career plans.

There was no way this wouldn't work.

Now if she could just head off this lawsuit, she'd be a happy woman.

"Let's hope third time is the charm," Dani said as Travis pulled up and parked in front of several buildings. One was a ranch-style house with brightly colored flowers planted in front. Beside it was a long, white building that she guessed was the kennel.

When they got out of the car, the sound of barking was almost deafening. No wonder Sarah lived so far off the beaten path. She had to. No neighbor would put up with the noise.

They headed toward the house first, but an elderly woman stepped out of the long building on the side and waved at them. As they walked over to join her, Dani couldn't help but get her hopes up. This woman looked happy and settled and not at all amazed by love.

"So glad you found us," Sarah said, shaking Dani's hand. "My husband, Ron, said you would get lost because I forgot a couple of steps in those directions I gave you." She smiled and added, "But I had faith in Freda's granddaughter. I knew you'd find your way."

Dani returned her smile and admitted, "I wish I could take credit, but Travis found the place. I wasn't of any help."

"That's not true. Your presence in the car helped me find the way," Travis said with a grin. "I couldn't have done it without you. We make a good team. Maybe we should hire ourselves out to help lost travelers."

Yup. Travis was definitely the same goof she'd known in high school. She liked that. She liked how they'd picked up their friendship as though school had been yesterday.

"Come in. I want you to meet my husband and my granddaughter. I've told them a lot about Freda over the years, and I'm sure up until now they thought I was making her up," Sara said. "Freda is quite a character."

"That she is," Dani said as she and Travis followed Sarah inside. The front part of the building was a vet's office, with exam rooms and a waiting area.

"What do you do here?" she asked.

"One of my daughters is a veterinarian, and she has her practice here. It's closed today, but normally the place is mobbed."

Sarah continued to the back of the building, which looked like a small hospital. They headed down the main aisle, stopping by the last room. Inside the room were a tall older man and a teenaged girl. Settled on a padded doggie bed were a glorious black Labrador retriever and a swarm of puppies.

Sarah walked over to the man, who slipped one arm around her waist. "This is my husband, Ron." She reached out and patted the teenaged girl's shoulder. "And this lovely lady is Lauren, my granddaughter. This is Dani and Travis."

Ron leaned forward and shook both of their hands. "It's nice to meet you, but you've ruined my ability to tease my wife that she's making up your grandmother. Seriously, does she really go around cursing people?"

Dani laughed, immediately liking this family. "Sorry to spoil your fun, but my grandmother is very much real. And I apologize for the curse on your wife."

"Didn't seem to hurt her," he said, giving Sarah a quick kiss on the forehead.

"What is this curse supposed to have done?" Lauren asked, her expression mischievous. "Is Grandma going to go nuts or grow fur on her back?"

Sarah pretended offense. "Hey."

"Yeah, hey," Ron said. "She's already done those things."

Everyone laughed, including Sarah, who gave her husband a playful tap on the arm.

"Now you see why I love this man," she said. "He makes me laugh."

Dani could easily see the deep love in this family.

They might joke and tease, but only as one more way to show their affection.

"My grandmother told your grandmother that love would always amaze her," Dani explained to Lauren, starting to think this was finally a curse recipient who might end the lawsuit. "But that could mean anything, right? Most of us find love amazing."

Lauren looked at her grandmother. "Is that where you got the name?"

Dani froze. Any positive thoughts she was having suddenly vaporized. "The name?"

Pride was in Ron's voice when he said, "Didn't my wife tell you? She breeds dogs."

"Yes. Certain breeds," Travis said. "For charities."

"That's right. Grandma breeds dogs to help disabled children," Lauren said, flashing her grandmother a grin. "Not only do they supply the children with companionship and devotion, they also perform many of the tasks the children need done on a daily basis. It helps them become independent. Grandma's phenomenal."

"Not me," Sarah said. "The *dogs* are phenomenal. They deserve all the credit."

Although personally, Dani found what Sarah did terrific, she also realized that the way things were going, she might as well tell her grandmother to pull out her checkbook.

"This sounds wonderful," Dani said, glancing at Travis. She could tell he hadn't seen this coming any more than she had.

"Is this company new?" Travis asked.

"Yes. I called it Amazing Love," she said. "And I swear, I wasn't thinking about your grandmother when I came up with the name. I've just always found the love these animals show to the children to be…amazing."

"Oh," was all Dani could think to say. This was unbelievable.

Sarah glanced at the dog with her puppies, and then smiled at Dani. "Do you realize that in a way, your grandmother's curse came true? I have found amazing love, in more ways than one. Not only the amazing love of my family, but also of these wonderful animals."

One of the hardest things Dani had ever done was return Sarah's smile. Sure, she was thrilled that this nice woman had a loving family and a wonderful business that helped children in need, but a tiny part of Dani wanted to stomp her feet and scream "no!"

She quickly got that tiny childish part of herself under control and managed a fairly decent smile at Sarah.

"It's funny how it worked out," Dani said, glancing at Travis. He gave her a sympathetic look, but she could also clearly see from his expression that he didn't consider this the end of the world.

And he was right. This was a setback, but the important thing was, despite her grandmother's curses coming true, or maybe because of them, all of these people were happy.

She took a deep breath and settled her emotions. Okay, so this hadn't worked, but she was a good lawyer. She could work out some sort of settlement with this man to stop the lawsuit and prevent her grandmother from getting financially drained.

These people were happy and that was what really mattered. And maybe Travis was right—maybe that was the bargaining chip she'd use. Every person her grandmother had cursed was better off because of the curse. That man must have done something to mess up his curse, otherwise he'd be happy like everyone else.

It was worth a shot.

For the next hour, Dani let herself enjoy her visit with Sarah and her family. She and Travis toured the impressive facility, seeing where the dogs were trained. It was, as Sarah said, an example of amazing love.

When they were about to leave, Dani stopped to give Freda's phone number and address to Sarah. When she turned back around, she saw Travis stuff several twenty-dollar bills in the donation box near the front door. He did it subtly, obviously not wanting anyone to see what he'd done.

And something tightened in Dani's chest. Travis Walker was a genuinely nice guy. She'd always known that, even in high school she'd known he was nice. He might come across to some women as all flirt and no substance, but she'd always seen the person under the persona.

A person who meant a great deal to her.

"I hope you'll come back and visit," Sarah said, shaking their hands once more. "And tell Freda I'll be in touch. It's been far too long since we talked. You should never lose touch with your oldest friends."

Dani didn't bother to point out that the women hadn't spoken in almost fifty years. The way her grandmother told the story, she had stopped by Sarah's house to talk about a boy she liked, and when Sarah had admitted she liked him as well, an argument had broken out.

Naturally, Freda maintained the fight wasn't at all her fault, but Dani suspected her grandmother had started it. Anyway, the end result was that the friendship had been destroyed and Freda had put the curse on Sarah.

"Yes, I'll have her call you," Dani said. "Also, do you have some brochures about your business? I know a lot of lawyers with way too much money on their hands, and Amazing Love looks like a perfect tax deduction to me."

Sarah laughed and handed Dani a handful of brochures. "We get a lot of our funding from people looking for a non-controversial tax deduction, which is fine by me. Money keeps this place going and I welcome all of it."

Dani tucked the brochures in her purse. Later, she'd drop her own check into the mail for Sarah, but like Travis, she didn't want thanks for giving. She simply wanted to help. She was sincerely in awe of the good Sarah was accomplishing.

As they headed toward the car, Dani glanced at Travis. He smiled at her, but it wasn't his usual lady-killer smile. He seemed as touched by what they'd just seen as she was.

She waited until they were both settled in the car and Travis had started driving before she said what she knew he was dying to say, "At least she's happy."

Travis chuckled. "Since you're the one pointing that out this time, I take it you've decided to use that as the defense."

Dani sighed. "I know when I'm beat. We gave it a good try, but let's face it, Freda's curses do come true. We talked to three people who were cursed for different reasons and in each case, the curse came true. There's no way I can use any of these people."

"We could talk to some more," Travis offered, turning on to the main road that fronted Sarah's property.

"Do you honestly think we'll find anything different?" Dani asked, curious as to what he thought. Maybe she'd made up her mind too quickly. Maybe he didn't see what she saw—a lost cause.

For a few seconds, he didn't say anything, and Dani found herself holding her breath.

Then he said, "I think you're right. I'm not into magic, and I really don't think Freda has magical powers. But it does seem like her curses do influence the recipients. Maybe on some subconscious level, they do what she said would happen in the curse. I don't know how they work, but they work."

"I don't know either," Dani admitted. "I'm really not sure why whatever Freda says seems to come true. I agree with you, I'm not a believer in magic and I really don't think my grandmother is some sort of witch. But I can't explain how all these people end up with lives that mirror what she said. All I know is, I can't use them to head off a lawsuit, and so I'm going to see what sort of settlement I can arrange."

Travis glanced at her. "I don't think you should offer him money. What kind of person blames a curse for his bad luck? This guy needs to take responsibility for his own actions and not blame his problems on your grandmother."

Dani had expected him to agree with her, so his reaction caught her by surprise. "I agree, but what else can I do? I can't use any of the people we've met this week to prove that their lives weren't impacted by what Nana said. If I don't offer him something, he's going to file suit, and we've got nothing if it goes to court."

"But you can bring these people into court and show how their lives were *improved* by what your grandmother said, and that his life would have been improved, too, if he hadn't done something to screw it up," Travis said. "Don't let him win, Dani. It's wrong."

Dani realized he had an excellent point, and a new idea started forming in her mind. "Any chance you can find out what exactly happened to his business? I mean, something must have happened to cause him to lose everything. So what was that something? I realize he started focusing on that woman and stopped paying attention, but what exactly happened? Did he stop coming to work so the store wasn't open? What?"

Travis flashed her a grin. "Now that's an idea I like. I'll get started right away. Shouldn't take too long to find out what this guy did wrong to send his business down the tubes."

For the first time in several days, Dani felt optimistic. This sounded like an excellent plan, and she was sure she could find out something that would help them. She smiled back at Travis, and wasn't surprised when attraction slammed into her like a tornado.

Last night had been fantastic. She's always enjoyed sex before, but sex with Travis was a whole new experience. He not only took her breath away, he made sex fun.

So much fun that she could hardly wait to do it again. Maybe, if he wasn't busy tonight…

"So what happens now?" he asked, almost as if he'd read her thoughts.

She blinked, and tried to focus on what they'd been discussing. "I guess we should head home and tell my grandmother what we're going to do."

Travis shot her a devilish look. "Okay. And then after that? I don't know about you, but I'd kind of like to get some more exercise. Guess I should be a little more subtle, but hey, subtle isn't my strong suit."

Dani laughed, thrilled he felt the same way about last night as she did. As excitement curled inside her, she said, "No, you're not exactly Mr. Subtle, but that's the great thing about being friends with benefits. You don't have to be subtle. We can be ourselves. We can say what we think."

When she didn't say anything else, he asked, "Okay, so what do you think about getting more exercise?"

"It sounds like an excellent idea to me," she admitted. "A truly excellent idea."

8

TRAVIS LOOKED at the smug expression on Freda's face and bit back a smile. The older woman was obviously delighted to learn that despite their best efforts, Dani and he had been unable to prove her "romantic suggestions" didn't work.

He knew Dani had been reluctant to come and speak to her grandmother for that very reason. But after they'd stopped by their apartments so they could each change their clothes, they'd come over to Dani's parents' house to face the music.

And now, Freda was enjoying this. She sat, very regally, on the couch next to Dani, and literally beamed at him.

"Ha! I told you my suggestions work," Freda said, her grin as bright as the full moon outside. She leaned over and patted Dani's hands. "I wouldn't make the suggestions if they didn't work, but I appreciate you trying to help me."

"I'll admit, for some reason, your romantic suggestions do seem to invoke some sort of subconscious power," Dani said. "So the bottom line is, we need to take another approach to prevent this lawsuit."

Freda waved both of her hands and shook her head. "What do you mean by subconscious? Are you saying you still don't believe in what I do? Didn't you just admit that they work? It has nothing to do with their subconscious. It has to do with reality." She looked from Dani to Travis then back to Dani. "You must have seen how powerful my romantic suggestions are. They are magical. And they work."

Travis watched in fascination as Dani carefully chose her words. He could clearly see how much she loved her grandmother and didn't want to hurt her, but he also knew Dani truly didn't believe in the magic of Freda's suggestions.

"I'll admit, your romantic suggestions had a powerful influence on these people's lives," she said, leaning over and patting her grandmother's hands. "And I know you must be thrilled to learn that these people are very happy and remember you fondly."

"Because of what I did," Freda said, looking at him for confirmation. "They like me because of what I did, right, Travis? They are happy because my romantic suggestions came true and changed their lives."

Man, talk about a dangerous situation. Freda was looking at him with expectation while Dani was frowning at him. For a moment, the right thing to do totally escaped him. Then his survival instincts kicked in and his brain finally managed to formulate an answer.

"From what I saw, your romantic suggestions had a huge impact on these people's lives," he said, not clarifying how he thought this impact happened.

"Each of them is happy and said to thank you for what you did."

There. He'd danced around her questions very adeptly if he did say so himself.

Freda once again got that cat-who-ate-the-canary expression on her face and turned to her granddaughter. "You may not be able to admit you believe in what you saw because it's how you were raised, but in my heart I'm sure you know that I caused those people to be happy. My romantic suggestions are powerful, and when I make one, people's lives change."

Conflicting emotions crossed Dani's pretty face. Travis could tell she was torn between saying what her grandmother wanted to hear and what she felt was the truth. One of the many things he admired about Dani was how much she cared for her grandmother. Dani was a woman with a heart.

A heart he only hoped remained untouched when their time together was over. As much as she kept saying the whole "friends with benefits" thing worked well for her, he also knew she was the type to fall in love.

And that worried him. The last thing he wanted to do was hurt Dani.

But right now, looking at Dani, she seemed fine. She didn't strike him at all as a woman suffering from a broken heart. In fact, what she struck him as was someone trying to escape a verbal trap.

"So you believe a little, right?" Freda asked Dani,

still trying to force an admission from her reluctant granddaughter.

In a move Travis could only describe as inspired, Dani leaned forward and hugged her grandmother.

"I love you. You're a terrific woman with many, many talents," Dani said.

Travis softly chuckled. Way to avoid answering the question. The woman was obviously an excellent lawyer.

Freda's knowing smile made it clear she was well aware of what her granddaughter was doing, but she let it go. She patted Dani's cheek and asked, "So what do we do now? I refuse to give Carl any of my money. What other options do we have?"

Travis leaned forward. "Dani and I think we can show that he did something that prevented his curse...I mean, his romantic suggestion from taking force."

Freda nodded. "He did mess it up. He didn't understand, and that's why his business went down the drain. It's not my fault that he got involved with some floozy who didn't really love him."

She leaned back against the sofa cushion and proclaimed, "Love is serious business. Carl should have shown it proper respect."

"Yes, he should have," Travis agreed. "But I guess he learned his lesson. That will teach him to mess around with love."

Freda raised one eyebrow and gave Travis a direct, unwavering look. "So I take it from what you just said that you and Dani aren't going to be foolish about what's happening between the two of you. You're going to show the love between you proper respect and not going to behave like fools, right?"

Surprised, Travis looked at Dani, who seemed as unnerved by her grandmother's comment as he was. He hadn't realized the change in their relationship was that obvious. Apparently it was, since Freda had had no trouble figuring out what was going on.

Dani cleared her throat. Then she cleared it a second time when her grandmother shifted her attention to her. Travis could tell Dani was wrestling with the right thing to say to her grandmother, but how did you explain friends with benefits to a woman who believed in life-long love?

Personally, he couldn't think of a thing to say, so he kept his mouth shut and waited for Dani's response.

Finally, with a laugh, she stood. "We've got a lot of work to do. Travis and I will get back in touch with you once we've worked out a new plan."

Freda stood and hugged her granddaughter. "I'll let you run away from me, but remember, you can't run away from yourself. And you certainly can't run away from love."

She turned toward Travis. "Love isn't something you treat lightly," she told him. When he started to respond, she held up one hand. "Even if you don't recognize love, it recognizes you."

With that pronouncement, Freda swept out of the living room, leaving Dani and Travis staring after her.

For a couple of seconds, neither of them said a word. What was there to say? They both had agreed emotions wouldn't get tangled up in what was happening with them, but could you always guarantee that?

So, in an attempt to lighten the mood, Travis said, "Well, I guess we've been warned."

But rather than laughing, Dani merely nodded. "Yes, we have. Let's just hope she's not right."

TALKING TO HER grandmother had been like facing an angry judge, Dani decided as she and Travis left her parents' house. Her grandmother was a strong-willed woman who saw the world her own special way and thought everyone else should see it that way as well.

But Dani didn't. She wasn't a big believer in love. Why would she be? Her parents certainly weren't a good example of a loving couple, and of the friends she had who'd married, several of them were already divorced.

As far as her own relationships went, she'd really liked all of her boyfriends, but she'd never felt anything remotely like love.

So how did you believe in something you'd never seen?

"I need to stop by the office," Travis said as they climbed in his car. "Want to come with me or do you want me to drop you at your apartment?"

"There's no reason for me to go there again," Dani said. "This afternoon when we stopped by so I could change clothes, I found it depressing with all the moving boxes."

That was only part of the reason why she wanted to hang around with Travis, and it was a very small part. The main reason was that she had her hopes set on a repeat of what had happened last night. It had been a long time since she'd had sex, and quite frankly, she'd never had sex like she'd had last night.

So a repeat sounded like an excellent idea. But even though Travis had said before they'd talked to Freda that he was interested in a repeat, she still wasn't sure that's what he wanted. At the moment, she couldn't tell if he wanted to be with her again or if he'd been hoping she'd want him to drop her off. All that talk about love might have changed his mind.

When they reached the offices of Walker Investigations, the young man she'd met the last time, Elvin Richards, was talking on the phone when they entered.

"So then the bad guy told Spiderman…" Elvin turned bright red at the sight of Travis and after a lot of muttering and mumbling said into the phone, "Mr. Max Walker isn't here at the moment, but I'll be happy to take a message if you'd like."

Rather than being upset, Travis chuckled and looked at Dani. "Makes you wonder what a superhero would want with Max. My brother is a great guy, but he can hardly leap tall buildings or spin webs. Now if they'd been asking to see me, well it would have been more believable."

Dani smiled, happy to see Travis wasn't going to yell at Elvin. She knew the young man wasn't the best employee, but she got the sense that he was trying in his own way.

"So you consider yourself tough enough to help out a superhero?" she teased.

Travis gave her a sexy look that made tingles dance across her skin. Leaning close to her, he softly said, "I think I did a fairly good job last night."

Normally, Dani considered herself a woman in control of her emotions, but at that moment, the air whooshed out of her lungs, and all she wanted to do was jump Travis. Just like that. She wanted him with an intensity that startled her. She'd never been someone fixated with sex, but today, there was nothing else she could think about.

"What if I say I can't remember?" She met his gaze.

"Then I'll be happy to provide a refresher," he said, his gaze dropping to her lips.

Lust seared through Dani like a flame, and she knew now beyond a shadow of a doubt that he was as interested in a repeat as she was.

"Sounds great," she said simply. The air between them crackled with awareness.

Travis looked as if he was about to say more when Elvin hung up the phone.

"Um, they didn't want to leave a message," he told Travis.

Travis turned to look at the young man, and Dani

found herself resenting the interruption. The sooner they got out of here and to Travis's apartment, the happier she'd be.

And apparently, she wasn't the only one who felt that way, because Travis started rushing through the office, checking the mail and the phone messages at record speed.

"Where's the fire?" Elvin finally asked. "Do you have an appointment?"

Travis glanced briefly at Dani, and then said, "Yes, we do."

He held up a stack of messages. "Are these all the phone calls? Anything else?"

Elvin shifted the pencils on his desk from one side to the other, and suddenly seemed to find the calendar on his desk fascinating.

Oh dear. This didn't look good.

"Elvin, what happened?" Travis asked, and although his voice and expression seemed calm, Dani knew he was trying hard not to lose his patience.

Elvin looked up. "Oh, did I tell you Max called? He asked me to tell you he and his wife are coming home from their honeymoon."

Travis flipped through the messages. "I don't see a note about his call. Did he say anything else? Does he want me to pick them up at the airport?"

"I'm positive he didn't want you to. Well, pretty positive," Elvin said. Once again, he looked down at his desk. The poor kid was obviously scared to tell Travis what had happened.

Dani couldn't blame Travis for being upset. This was a business after all, and it was important that telephone calls be returned and messages not be lost. She'd probably lose her cool if her secretary messed up her messages.

But Travis didn't. Instead, he said, "Just tell me what happened, Elvin. Bad news doesn't get better with time."

Elvin finally looked up. "It wasn't my fault. Not really. I was doing what you told me to do."

Travis nodded. "So somehow it was my fault. Ah, well in that case, I apologize. Now, what exactly did I do?"

Elvin looked baffled. "No, I didn't mean it was your fault, like you had done it or something." He thought for a second and then added, "But you did tell me to empty the trash whenever the basket got full, so in a way, I guess it is your fault. And how was I supposed to know that my notes had fallen into the basket?"

Oh no. The young man had thrown Travis's messages in the trash and then emptied it. Dani looked at Travis, knowing he must want to explode.

But he didn't. He sighed. Then he sighed again. Then he said, "Elvin, from now on, answer the phone and if callers want to leave a message, transfer them to my voice mail."

The young man obviously didn't know he'd been skating on thin ice because rather than thanking Travis for not firing him, he said, "That's a good idea, because truthfully, I'm too busy to keep taking all these messages."

Travis rubbed one hand across his face, then turned away from Elvin. Dani knew he'd pretty much had all he could take, so she walked over and patted his arm.

"Those people will call back," she assured him.

"Probably. But I wonder how thrilled Max is going to be if I'm supposed to pick him up," he pointed out.

"Like I said, I'm pretty positive he doesn't want you to get him," Elvin said with a big smile. "I wouldn't worry about it."

Travis made a soft groaning noise, and Dani could tell he was rapidly reaching the end of his rope. Jumping in, she told Elvin to have a nice evening, and then she tugged on Travis's arm until she got him out of the office.

When they were in the hallway, he sighed. "I need to fire that kid."

"No you don't. And you won't. You're too nice for that," she said, tucking her arm through his as they walked to the exit. "You're a very nice man."

Travis raised one eyebrow. "You think I'm nice? I'm not sure how I feel about that."

"Of course I think you're nice," she said, bumping him with her hip as they walked. "It's one of the many, many things I like about you."

They'd reached the parking lot, and as they crossed over to his car, Travis said, "Well, I think you're nice, too. And it's one of the many, many things I like about you."

As silly and goofy as it seemed, Dani enjoyed his compliment, and even though he was only repeating back to her what she'd said to him, it didn't matter. She felt warm and happy simply because Travis had told her she was nice and that he liked her.

Could she be any more juvenile?

Apparently so, because when he went on to explain that he liked her because she was kind to people, she actually blushed.

"Okay, I think you need to stop saying nice things to me now," she said, patting her cheeks. "I seem to have lost my mind temporarily and can't take much more."

Travis opened her car door and dropped a light kiss on her lips. "I like making you blush."

Dani smiled. "Really? Well, you won't find many things that work."

"Odd that compliments do," he noted. "It makes me sad to think you haven't had a lot of experience with them."

He was right about that. Growing up in her household, compliments were scarce. And now at the law firm, they were even scarcer. Of course, Freda gave her compliments, but when she thought about it, she couldn't think of anyone else who did.

"Not all of us are told on a regular basis how wonderful we are," she teased, wanting to lighten the mood. "I imagine you hear that quite often."

"Sometimes, but it's usually in a breathless, female voice." He flashed her his bad-boy grin and added, "Sort of like the one you used last night."

Dani laughed and climbed into his car. "You're unbelievable."

"Yeah, I hear that one a lot, too." He shut her car door and left her laughing inside as he walked around to the driver's side.

Once he was settled in the car, Dani said, "I'm going to miss you."

He seemed surprised by what she'd said, but he couldn't be as surprised as she was. She hadn't meant to say that, hadn't meant to say anything remotely like that.

But now that she'd said it, she realized it was true. She was going to miss him for a lot of reasons.

Rather than joke, he said, "I'm going to miss you, too."

"I haven't laughed this much since high school," she admitted.

"Me, neither." He put the key in the ignition, but he didn't start the car. Instead, he sat looking out the windshield and a sad sort of silence fell over them.

Dani cleared her throat and said the first thing that popped in her mind. "I'm hungry."

Travis laughed and looked at her. "Want to come to dinner at my place? I'm not the best cook in the world, but I'm also not the worst."

"You sure about that?" she teased. "What proof do you have?"

"No one I've fed has ever died," he said proudly.

Dani pretended to consider his statement. "That's pretty strong evidence in your favor, I'll admit."

"So is that a yes?" He grinned that sexy, crooked grin that Dani absolutely loved.

That was one more thing about him she was going to miss. No other man could make her heart race and her palms sweat with just one sexy look, but Travis could turn her on with a simple smile.

"I would love to come to dinner," she said, leaning back in her seat as he started the car.

Then he flashed her another grin. Oh, yes, she was going to miss that grin. It made her mind go blank. Well, sort of blank. She did think about one thing— how much she wanted Travis.

She considered whether she should mention to him that she was hoping for a lot more than simply food tonight, but she figured that went without saying. He knew how much she wanted him.

On the way to his apartment, Dani kept up a steady stream of chatter about the case and how she thought they could handle their argument. Although Travis murmured agreements at the appropriate places, she got the definite feeling he wasn't completely listening to her.

"So then an elephant sat on my head and messed up my hair," she said.

"That's nice." Travis pulled into a garage and parked the car.

"You're not listening to me," she pointed out. "Is something wrong?"

After Travis turned off the car, he looked at her. "Sorry about that. Guess my mind was on something else."

He looked so handsome, so sexy, that Dani couldn't resist leaning over and kissing him. Her action obviously startled him because for a second he sat perfectly still.

Then, as if a dam had broken, he kissed her back with such intensity, such depth, it literally took her breath away.

Dani had no idea how long they sat in his car kissing, but it was a long, long time. One kiss led to another, each lasting longer than the one before. Travis seemed as hungry for her as she was for him. They were acting as if it had been months since they'd been together instead of hours.

She couldn't get enough of him, and kissing in the car was frustrating. She couldn't get as close as she wanted.

Finally, Dani pulled back and rested her forehead against his. "Wow," was all she could manage to say.

Travis chuckled softly. "Yes, wow." After a second, he said, "That's why I was distracted in the car. I was thinking about what might happen tonight... between us."

Dani smiled, even though she knew Travis couldn't see it in the darkness of the car. "That's why I was chattering. I was thinking about the same thing."

Then he kissed her neck, leaving a trail of warmth behind. Dani tipped her head and closed her eyes, giving herself over to the sensations he was evoking.

"I want to make your fantasies come true," he murmured as he continued his exploration of her skin. "Tell me your fantasies. What makes you crazy?"

Dani struggled to form a cohesive sentence, but it was difficult with the magic he was creating around them.

"I'm okay. This is good," Dani finally managed to say, her voice breathless and heavy with the want humming through her veins.

He slowly unbuttoned the top two buttons on her blouse, his fingers flicking them open with practiced skill. Then he parted the material and slipped his oh-so-talented fingers under the material. With leisurely finesse, he traced the lace decorating her bra.

"Do you like this?" he asked softly.

When she murmured an agreement, he softly brushed her lips with his as he rubbed her bud-tight nipples through the fabric. "You must have some fantasies, Dani. Tell me what they are."

She drew a deep breath into her lungs as he tugged on the tips of her nipples, desire shooting through her and pooling low in her womb.

"We could always play the maiden and the pirate," he teased as he circled her nipples with his thumbs. "That could be a lot of fun."

Deciding two could play at this game, Dani

wrapped her arms around his neck, pulling him closer. She nibbled on his earlobe and whispered, "You're too scruffy to be a maiden."

Travis chuckled and kissed her again. This time the kiss was longer than before, and deeper. He leisurely explored her mouth with his tongue, then nibbled on her bottom lip.

"So I guess the sheriff and the schoolmarm is out for the same reason," he said as he broke off the kiss and refocused his attention on her breasts.

"Hmmm," she said as he again tugged lightly on her nipples.

In the muted light of the car, she watched as he licked one fingertip, then dipped his hand beneath her bra and circled her nipple. The coolness of his finger against her overheated skin made Dani mew softly with pleasure.

"Let's play the detective and the lawyer," he murmured in her ear. "I think we'd be good at that."

Dani nodded. "Okay. Let's go do that now. Right now. This very second."

"In a rush, are you?"

She pulled his hand out from under her blouse, rebuttoned it, then shoved open her car door.

"Yes. I'm in a big rush," she told him as she climbed out of the car. "This lawyer can't wait to see how you hold up under examination."

Travis got out of the car and locked it. As he walked over to join her, he teased, "And this private detective can hardly wait to thoroughly investigate you."

9

Dani couldn't say which of them was in the bigger rush to reach the sanctuary of Travis's apartment. As far as she could tell, both of them were moving at the speed of light. Well, except for those moments when passion would overcome one of them and they'd stop for some serious necking to tide them over.

But finally, thankfully, they reached his apartment. Dani tugged Travis's shirt free from his pants while she waited for him to unlock the door.

"What's taking you so long?" she teased, sliding one hand under his shirt and caressing the warm, muscled skin of his back. Touching him like this, and having the freedom to touch him, only added to the excitement bubbling inside her. "It's almost like you're not focused on your task."

Travis made a half-groan, half-growl noise that promised retribution once they got inside. Dani found the idea of retribution—at least the type she knew he had in mind—delightfully blissful. Just the thought of what he might do made her already racing pulse kick into an even higher gear.

She imagined him doing something similar to her,

pulling her shirt from her slacks, running his hands across her skin, lingering to touch and fondle and excite. When he reached her bra, he'd take his time. He'd skim his finger across her hard nipples, plucking them through the silk material as he had in the car. Perhaps he'd lean down and take one taut nipple in his mouth and suckle it through the material while she held on to him for dear life. And then he'd—

"Stop that right now!"

The startled exclamation from across the hall ripped Dani's fantasy into tiny pieces. She yanked her hand out from under Travis's shirt and turned to face the person behind her.

A tiny elderly man with tufts of white hair and enormous glasses stood staring at them. He blinked several times, the enormous glasses making his brown eyes look enormous as well. Then he crumpled his face into a deep frown.

"Travis Walker, you need to control yourself," the man said. "This is a public hallway. Women and children walk through this hallway. What would they think if they saw you and your lady friend acting like this?"

Travis turned around and then glanced at Dani. She could tell he wanted to laugh, but the expression on his face was nothing but sincere when he answered the man's accusation.

"Mr. Bryant, I wasn't doing anything except trying to get the door to my apartment open," Travis explained. "It was my lady friend who was acting outrageously. I'm with you. She needs to learn to keep her hands to herself. I'll have a stern talk with her once we get inside."

Dani looked at him and rolled her eyes. What a liar.

But when she turned her gaze back to the elderly man, he seemed to be buying the bunk Travis was selling. He was giving her a condemning look.

"You need to learn some self-control, young lady," the elderly man said. Then, with a huff and one more scathing look, he headed down the hall, leaving Dani and Travis staring after him.

Once the elderly man was in the elevator, Dani looked at Travis. He grinned and she nudged him with her elbow.

"You are a rat," she said, trying not to laugh, but not really succeeding when he gave her an innocent look.

"What did I do? I simply told Mr. Bryant the truth. You were the one groping me."

Rather than point out that she knew for a fact he was as interested in groping her as she was in groping him, Dani decided to take a different approach. Leaning against him, she stood on tiptoe and nibbled on his earlobe. When he didn't immediately fall for her plan, she tried something guaranteed to insure success.

"I want you naked," she whispered in his ear.

Travis groaned softly, and then obviously accepting his defeat, he slipped one arm around her waist and tugged her even closer.

"Did you get that door unlocked yet?" she asked, her own voice husky with desire.

Although she'd planned on teasing him some more, being this close to Travis made it impossible for Dani to think about anything but being with him.

"If it's not unlocked, I'll kick it in," he murmured, trying the handle again. This time, she noted thankfully, the door was unlocked and Travis was able to simply push it open.

Dani grabbed one of his hands and tugged him inside, then slammed the door behind them.

"Lock it," she told him.

Travis raised one eyebrow, but did as she'd ordered. "Feeling bossy tonight?"

"Empowered," she said, and then she reached out and flicked open several buttons on his shirt. "Are you okay with that?"

His grin made it clear he thought it was a fantastic idea, but rather than asking, he replicated her actions, opening the buttons on her blouse. His technique, though, was a lot sneakier than hers. Each time he slipped a button free, he took the opportunity to let his fingers caress the skin he'd exposed underneath. The sensation of his warm hands on her body brought all the passion they'd shared earlier in his car flooding back to her.

She closed her eyes, letting the memories wash over her. Desire flared again inside her as he ran his hands across her abdomen.

How did Travis manage to do this? How could he get her this turned on with just a touch? She'd never considered herself an overly sensual person. Sure, she enjoyed sex, but she'd never been as wild, as consumed as she was when she was with Travis.

"Open your eyes," he murmured.

Dani did. Once her gaze locked with his, he undid the front fastening of her bra. Without breaking eye contact, he slipped the material off her sensitive skin, and then ran his hands over her breasts. Dani sucked in a tight breath and was about to close her eyes again when he shook his head slowly.

"I want us to experience this together," he said. "I want to look into your eyes as I touch your body."

Dani felt her breath catch in her throat at his seductive suggestion. She would have said something, but as he caressed her breasts, coherent thought was out of the question.

She wouldn't have thought looking at him while he touched her would make her feel so close to him, but it did. She felt connected in a way that went far beyond merely being touched by his hands; it felt as if he'd touched her with his soul.

Her emotions were in turmoil as he lightly brushed his fingers over her nipples. He was seducing her mind along with her body.

"I want you to remember tonight, Dani," he said. "After you move to New York, I want this memory to last for you."

"Um, okay," she said, knowing she should be a heck of a lot more eloquent than that, but incapable of eloquence at the moment.

"If there's anything you'd like me to do, anything you really enjoy, let me know," he said.

If she hadn't been looking him directly in the face, she might have thought he was teasing her. But he was sincere, and if her body hadn't been on fire with desire for him, she might have told him how touched she was by his request.

Instead, as each tantalizing second passed, all she could think about was how much she wanted Travis. When he tugged on her nipples, something inside her snapped.

"Now. What I want is you, now," she said, reaching out and snagging him around the neck. She pulled his head down and kissed him hard, her tongue sliding deep within his mouth.

As they kissed, she pushed and pulled frantically at his clothing. Travis helped her, not only with his clothes, but hers as well.

He did manage to ask once, "Do you want to move to the bedroom?"

Dani realized with a start that they were still standing in the living room of his apartment. But she didn't care. To her way of thinking, the bedroom was too far away.

"No, this is fine. I want you now," she told him, kissing his chest. "This is fine."

Travis moaned softly with desire, which she took as agreement. Then, when he started to slide off his boxers, a new idea occurred to her.

"No, let me," she said.

Travis smiled, his eyes filled with the fire burning inside him. "Okay."

Dani slipped her fingers under the waistband of his boxers and slowly pulled them down. Once she'd freed him, she ran her hands over his impressive length.

"Let's put that to good use," she teased.

The smile he gave her was full of heat and lust, but also something more. Something deeper that tugged on her heart. For a few precious seconds, she merely looked at him.

Then he took a deep breath and said, "I'm not sure how much more willpower I have, Dani."

She completely understood what he meant. "Now would be good."

Leaning over, he snagged his pants and pulled out his wallet.

"Condom," he muttered, removing the small packet.

Dani took it away from him and quickly covered him. Then she glanced around for a place to go, but Travis lifted her and backed her against the front door.

"Now would be very good," he said, helping her wrap her legs around his waist. With a quick thrust he entered her, and then they both gave themselves over to the waves of wildness overtaking them.

Dani clung to him, taking him deep into her body with each thrust. She'd never felt so free, so consumed by need as she did at this moment.

As the intensity of their lovemaking grew, Dani

felt release hover just beyond her grasp. Finally, with one last, deep thrust, Travis pushed her to the brink and then over the edge. He called out her name as he buried himself deep within her and found his own release.

Afterward, Travis held her for several long moments, his forehead resting against hers, both of them breathing hard.

Dani finally slipped her legs free of his waist and stood, although she was more than a little wobbly at first, so Travis put one arm around her waist to steady her.

"You okay?" he asked, his gaze tender as he brushed the hair out of her face. "I didn't hurt you, did I?"

Dani marveled at how he could be so insane with passion one moment and then so gentle and loving the next. The answer came to her like a flash of lightning—Travis was a special man. He was a man who could drive her wild with desire and make her laugh until her sides hurt, but he also was a man who was kind and caring.

Her earlier statement had been true—she really was going to miss him once she moved.

"Dani, are you okay?" he repeated when she didn't answer.

She could tell he was genuinely concerned that somehow he'd done something wrong, so she kissed him soundly, and then said, "I'm fine. More than fine. I've never had sex up against a door. I feel like a wanton woman."

Relief crossed his face. "Good. I was afraid I got a little carried away." He ran one hand across his face. "Up against the front door. I can't believe I did that to you."

"I loved it," she assured him, glancing around his living room. "In fact, let's see what other places in your apartment are great for sex."

At first, Travis seemed surprised by her comment. Then, he grinned his wicked, bad-boy grin and said, "Sounds like a good idea to me."

THE RINGING in his head went on and on. Travis forced himself to open his eyes even though that was the last thing he wanted to do.

"Make it stop," Dani murmured next to him.

She snuggled closer and he gave her a hug. "I will, as soon as I figure out what it is."

"Doorbell," she said with a sigh. "Tell them we're not interested."

Travis listened for a moment. Yeah, she was right. It was the doorbell. Who the hell would wake him up this early on a Saturday? He glanced at the clock. Okay, it was almost nine so it wasn't exactly the middle of the night.

Still, he was bone-tired and he didn't want to talk to whoever was at the door. When the ringing continued, he reluctantly left the warmth of the bed and Dani's body and stood.

Glancing around he saw no sign of his clothes and then remembered. He and Dani had made a thorough examination of his apartment last night. They'd made love on almost every available surface. It had been fun and crazy, and his apartment definitely showed signs of that experience.

If his memory was still intact, his clothes were right by the front door. That was convenient.

Padding over to the door, he snagged his boxers and had just slipped them on when someone started unlocking the door.

Damn, why hadn't he put the chain on the door last night as well as locking it. Travis reached out and slammed the door shut with one hand, holding it closed with some effort.

"What the hell do you think you're doing?" he yelled at whoever was on the other side. This better not be the landlord stopping by just to snoop.

"I'm checking on my little brother," the answer came back. "His car is downstairs, so I can't figure out why he isn't answering his door."

Max. Travis felt like an idiot. That's right, Max and his new wife, Paige, were due back in town today. He just hadn't expected them to stop by his apartment.

He cast a quick look at the living room. Although the sofa cushions were on the floor right next to the knickknacks from the coffee table, it didn't look too bad. Well, that was if you kept one eye closed.

When Max started shoving on the door again, Travis kicked his and Dani's clothes behind an over-stuffed chair, and then pulled open the door.

Max barreled into the room the way he did everything in life—with intensity. Although the timing stunk, Travis was glad to see him and returned the bear hug Max gave him.

"How you doing, Trav? Been taking good care of our clients?" Max asked.

Sometimes life refused to give a guy a break, because before Travis could say a word, Dani wandered out from the bedroom wearing one of his old T-shirts.

She skittered to a stop when she saw Max and Paige, then with a weak smile, said, "Oops."

Max looked from Dani to Travis then back at Dani. "Hello, Dani. How have you been? Haven't seen you since high school."

To give her credit, Dani regained her composure quickly. She extended her hand and shook Max's. "Good to see you again, Max. You look well. And the case is going fine. Travis is doing a wonderful job. I'm really pleased."

The second she said the last sentence, everyone froze. Travis rolled his eyes and said to his brother, "Shut up."

"I didn't say a word," Max said, although it was obvious he was trying not to laugh.

Travis turned to Paige, who was watching the whole scene with amusement equaling her husband's. "Hello, Paige. I don't know how you can stand that jerk of a brother of mine. You deserve so much better."

Paige laughed and went to stand by Max. "He's

not a jerk. He's just easily amused." She smiled at Dani and introduced herself. "I'm Paige Walker, Travis's sister-in-law."

After shaking hands, Dani said, "Dani Karlinski. My grandmother may be sued, so I'm trying to get her out of trouble. Travis is working for me."

This time, Max laughed loud and long. "Hey, I tried," he said when Travis shot him a dirty look. "But there's only so much a man can take."

Paige sighed and patted Max on the arm. "I'm going to take my husband here and we're going to go get breakfast, so you two can have a chance to…" She glanced at the living room then back at them. "A chance to wake up."

Then, without giving Max time to protest, she took his hand and said, "Come on. We'll go get food and then we'll bring it back."

With a sigh, Max followed her to the door. Right before he walked out, he looked at Travis. "While we're gone, don't do anything I wouldn't."

"In that case, there's a hell of a lot that I can do," Travis said.

Max would have said something else, but Paige tugged him through the front door, and then shut it behind them. Once his brother and his wife were gone, Travis turned to look at Dani.

"Sorry about that," he said.

He had no idea how she was going to react. A lot of women would have gotten upset, but after studying first the living room and then the T-shirt she was wearing, Dani looked at him and said with a laugh, "I think we made an impression on them."

Glad that she was okay, Travis smiled. That was another one of the things he liked about Dani. She always kept her cool.

"Yep, I don't think there's any doubt that at this moment, Max and Paige are talking about us."

Dani walked over and slipped her arms around his waist. "Will he get mad at you for having earth-shattering sex with a client?"

Travis chuckled and brushed a kiss across her lips. "He can't say a word even though he might want to. See, Paige was a client when he met her."

Dani flashed him a knowing smile. "Oh. Then you're right. He can't say a word." She glanced around the living room. "Any idea where my clothes are?"

Travis pulled their clothes out from behind the chair. "Sorry if they got wrinkled."

"No problem." She snuggled against him, and despite everything going on around them, he was immediately aroused.

"As much as I'd like to oblige," he told her, "we don't have enough time. We have to get dressed before my brother gets back."

She gave him a flirty, sexy look that did nothing to calm his libido. "I know. So I suggest that to save time we take our shower together."

Without waiting for an answer from him, she headed down the hallway toward the bathroom.

Knowing this might take a while, Travis locked the

front door and slipped the chain in place before following her.

Max and Paige would have to wait. A man had to have his priorities in this world.

"I THINK it's romantic that your grandmother makes people fall in love," Paige said as they all ate breakfast at the small dining room table in Travis's apartment.

Dani looked at the other woman. She liked Paige. She was kind and obviously hopelessly in love with her new husband.

"My grandmother doesn't really make people fall in love," Dani explained. "She makes what she calls romantic suggestions to these people, but I'm sure when she does these suggestions, the poor recipients feel as though they've been cursed rather than blessed."

Paige took a muffin from the plate of pastries she and Max had brought back to the apartment and said, "Maybe the people feel like that at first, but don't they fall in love afterward? Travis, didn't you say that they're all very happy? That doesn't sound like people who've been cursed."

"The three people we've talked to so far seem happy," Travis said, leaning back in his chair. "But Paige, that's the problem. We can't stop the suit if everyone is thrilled to have been cursed."

"I'm sorry it doesn't help the case, but I still think it's romantic," Paige said. "Your grandmother must be a special lady to be able to bring other people happiness. That's rare in this world."

Before Paige could wrap this whole idea up in pretty paper, Dani said, "I love my grandmother, but she doesn't have magical powers. The only power she has is the power of suggestion. I think when she places these romantic suggestions on people, they're so startled or surprised or freaked out that what she says sinks into their subconscious. Once it's there, they end up doing what she said they'd do."

Paige frowned, obviously not liking Dani's reality-based theory. "I don't agree. Didn't you say most of them didn't even remember what she'd said? If it's such an important part of their subconscious, you'd think they'd at least remember something about it."

The other woman had a point, but Dani didn't believe in magic. She didn't want to argue with Paige, so she said, "Well, whatever the reason, now I have to find a different way to help my grandmother. Travis is going to find out specifically what the man did wrong to cause his business to fail."

"Yeah, romantic or not, these people being madly in love doesn't help our case." Travis was sitting next to Dani and now she glanced at him. He looked so sexy and cute this morning, and despite what they'd shared an hour ago in the shower, she found herself wanting him again.

Max was out in the kitchen toasting a bagel and he started to curse. "Trav, what's wrong with this thing?" he hollered at his brother. "You need to buy a new toaster. This one is broken."

Travis sighed. "Excuse me," he said to Dani and

Paige, and then he headed toward the kitchen, muttering about bozo brothers as he went.

Once he was out of earshot, Paige said to Dani, "So tell me, when are you going to tell Travis you're in love with him?"

Dani froze. She couldn't have heard that right. "What?" she finally managed to say. "We're not in love. We're just friends. Close friends."

Paige didn't look convinced. In fact, she looked downright unconvinced. "Did your grandmother place a romantic suggestion on you and Trav?"

Staring at the other woman, Dani couldn't believe what she was saying. They weren't in love. Far from it. Sure, they liked each other. And sure, they had great sex. But that was it.

"No, she didn't place a romantic suggestion on us, but even if she had, it wouldn't have done a thing. More importantly, you're misreading us. Travis and I aren't in love." Dani said the last sentence firmly, wanting to make certain she didn't mislead the other woman.

Paige continued to look at her with a doubtful expression. Finally, she said, "Oh. I guess I did misread the signs. I thought the way you two looked at each other and held hands and shared smiles meant you were in love. Guess I'm wrong."

"Well, we do like each other and we are involved, but it's just short-term," Dani explained. "I'm moving to New York in less than a week to start a new job."

"Congratulations," Paige said. "Then I guess it's

a good thing you and Travis aren't in love. It would cause real problems when you move away. Long-distance relationships rarely work."

Dani would have answered her, but the fighting from the kitchen caused Paige to sigh and head off to help the men before they killed each other over the toaster.

Knowing they didn't need any additional help, Dani stayed behind at the small dining-room table. The view out the window was magnificent, but she hardly saw it.

Instead, she was thinking about what Paige had said. Did she and Travis really look at each other like people in love? She knew they laughed a lot and that they understood each other, but they'd been friends for a long time.

But liking someone and getting along with him didn't mean you were in love. It just meant you were friends. And in their case, friends with benefits.

She and Travis were nothing more. They weren't in love and they never would be. She was positive of that.

Wasn't she?

10

THE SECOND he stepped into the office on Monday morning, Travis knew he was in for a rough day. Not only were he and Dani meeting with Carl Whitley, the man who was considering suing her grandmother, but Max was already at work, and from the look on his face, an inquisition was about to happen.

"Hey, Trav. Did you have a nice weekend?" Max asked.

"Cut to the chase," Travis said. "Dani will be here in about an hour, so I don't have time for games."

"Okay, no games." Max folded his arms across his chest and leaned back against Elvin's desk. "What's going on with you and Dani?"

"You know what's going on with us. You saw it with your own eyes. Next question."

He'd hoped being direct with Max would wrap this up quickly, but no such luck. His brother looked like he was settled in for a long conversation.

"Paige thinks you two are in love," Max said. He raised one eyebrow. "What do you think?"

"We're not," Travis said. He and Dani had spent

the weekend together, and she had told him what Max's wife thought. "We're not interested in anything long-term, so drop it."

Deciding he was through with this conversation even if his brother wasn't, Travis headed toward his office. Why was it that people in love insisted the rest of the world be in love, too? Why couldn't they just leave everyone else alone?

But apparently they couldn't, since Max followed him into the office.

"You sure you're not in love with her?" Max sat in one of the chairs facing Travis's desk. "I didn't realize I was in love with Paige for a long time. You may be in love with Dani and not know it."

That stopped him. Travis leaned back in his chair and frowned at his brother. "No offense, but how in love could I be with Dani if I didn't know it? Aren't you supposed to be breathless and obsessed when you're in love? And don't you walk around annoying everyone you see by insisting they be in love, too?"

"Cute," Max said. "It's not like that."

Travis balled up an old memo and tossed it into the trash. "Could have fooled me, especially about the annoying part."

Rather than being offended, Max laughed. "Yeah, I guess I am kind of a convert. Up until I met Paige, I didn't believe in love. But I do now."

"But I don't, and I'm not," Travis pointed out. "It's terrific that you and Paige are happy, but I need you to back off. Dani has worked for years for this job in

New York. I want to focus on this agency. We're good, and we understand each other."

Max slowly nodded and then stood. "Message received. I'll leave you two alone and so will Paige. But I'm going to say one more thing to you and I want you to remember it—don't throw away something great just because you're too much of an idiot to appreciate it. Realize when you've found something special."

With that, he walked out of the office. Travis stared after him, half annoyed, half amused. Man, his brother sure had changed since meeting Paige. He wasn't even the same guy Travis had grown up with. He was different. Better in some ways, and yeah, maybe worse in some other ways. But definitely different.

Showed you what kind of trouble a man could get into when he started believing in love.

DANI SURVEYED the man across the table and formulated her plan. Carl Whitley was an unhappy person. Based on the wrinkles on his face, he'd always been an unhappy person. She half suspected he enjoyed being unhappy since he'd already complained about everything in his lawyer's meeting room right down to the carpeting.

No wonder he wanted to sue Freda. This man obviously liked to cause trouble.

Dani glanced at Travis, who was sitting on her right side. He'd dug up a lot of information about Carl's business, which was really going to help them.

Nana Freda sat on her other side. She was dressed in her fanciest dress, and even though Dani had suggested several times that a simple dress would work, Freda had insisted on what she called her "party gown."

On the other side of the conference table sat Carl Whitley and his lawyer, Roger Abner. Roger had been the one to call this meeting, saying that he thought Freda and Carl could work this out if they just sat down and talked.

Dani suspected the man had decided he couldn't win this case, so the best he could do was find some sort of settlement. That worked perfectly for Dani since she also didn't think it was possible to win this if they sued. So rather than a formal lawsuit, both sides had agreed to try to reach an agreement without this getting any messier.

"I want to start," Carl said loudly, too loudly for the small room. He shot a frown at Freda, who in turn, simply smiled at him. That made the blood vessels in his forehead stand out.

"I appreciate that you're willing to try to settle this," Roger said, glancing around the room. "If this became a lawsuit, it would take a long time to go to trial, and no one wants that expense."

"She can pay," Carl muttered. "She has money."

"No I don't. I've told you, my son has money. I don't." Freda leaned back in her chair. "You need to listen better. You should wear your hearing aid."

Dani looked at Travis, who seemed as surprised

as she was that Freda knew the man wore a hearing aid.

"I can hear just fine. And I don't think there's anything to talk about," Carl said. "She placed a curse on me and it ruined my business. Now she needs to pay."

Dani looked at her notes, and then asked, "Have you always believed in curses and magical spells?" She paused long enough to let him consider the question, and then she added, "You don't seem like the type to believe in the supernatural."

"I don't think Mr. Whitley is claiming to believe in the supernatural as much as he's saying it was unnerving," Roger said.

Wanting to hear what Carl actually felt, Dani looked directly at him. "So is that what you felt? Unnerved? Unnerved to the point where you started closing your shop early?"

Carl's face turned bright red. He looked like a tomato about to explode. "That woman pointed her ugly finger at me and cursed me."

"Calm down and drink some water before you have a stroke," Freda said, pushing the pitcher of water toward him. "Did you take your blood-pressure medicine today? I bet you didn't."

This time, everyone in the room looked at Freda.

"How do you know he takes blood pressure medicine?" Roger asked.

Freda laughed, which only seemed to annoy Carl more. "I've been going to his dry cleaners for fifteen years. We talked every time I was in there."

Dani turned her attention back to Carl. "If you've been talking for fifteen years, did you know about my grandmother's romantic suggestions?"

Her grandmother had told her that Carl did, but Dani wanted to hear what the man himself said. More than likely, he was going to deny it.

But instead, he said, "She mentioned them a few times. You know, in passing she'd say something."

"How did she explain them? What exactly did she say when you talked about these romantic suggestions?" Dani asked.

Carl blew out a loud breath. "I don't remember *exactly* what she said. But I knew what she meant. She was telling me she had a way to make people do what she wanted them to do by putting a spell on them."

That was what she wanted him to say. Dani glanced at her notes, letting Carl's words sink in for everyone in the room, and then she asked, "So you believed that these suggestions she made worked? You didn't tell Mrs. Karlinski that 'that's just a load of bunk' when she explained what she did?"

Carl suddenly made a big procedure out of pouring water into his glass. After that, he took a bottle of pills out of his pocket and fumbled with the lid. "I need to take my pill."

When he obviously wasn't going to get the medicine bottle opened anytime soon, Freda reached out her hand. "Give it to me. You never could open that thing. You should ask for the ones that aren't childproof."

To Dani's amazement, Carl handed the bottle to

Freda without comment. "The ones that aren't child-proof aren't safe."

Freda handed the now-open bottle back to Carl. "They're only not safe if you have small children in your house. You don't have small children or grand-children running around your place, Carl."

"I know, I know," Carl said, taking the bottle and getting his pill.

Dani glanced at Travis, who winked at her. Apparently he found the relationship between Freda and Carl as interesting as she did. They obviously had been friends for many years until the disagreement and despite their fight, still shared a certain intimacy.

Dani realized that she might have found something she could use in her favor. Carl and Freda had a history, and she might be able to draw on that.

After Carl had taken his pill, Dani repeated her question. "So did you think her suggestions worked or did you think they were bunk?"

Carl ran one hand through his thinning gray hair. "I might have said at first that I didn't believe in them. But she kept saying they worked, so when she cursed me—"

"Stop calling it a curse," Freda said with a huff. "It was a romantic suggestion, not a curse. I don't try to hurt people. I try to make them happy. You know I'd never hurt a soul, Carl."

"Felt like a curse," Carl muttered. "I couldn't believe you'd done it to me."

"Why? Why couldn't you believe she'd done this to you?" Dani prompted.

Carl looked visibly upset, and Dani couldn't understand why.

"Carl, you don't have to answer the question if you don't want to," Roger advised his client.

Carl sighed several times, and finally said, "I did believe what she said when she cur—I mean placed the romantic suggestion on me. The way she'd said it, I knew it was going to come true."

Hoping to clarify what had happened, Dani asked her grandmother, "So why did you place the romantic suggestion on Mr. Whitley? What did you think would happen?"

Freda smiled at the older man. "I wanted to make him happy. He was getting meaner and meaner over the years. The last time I was there, he ruined my dress—"

"I did not ruin your dress," Carl said. "It had rips in it when you dropped it off."

"Why would I bring a ripped dress to the dry cleaners?" She made a scoffing noise. "Pah. No one would do something so foolish."

"They would if they wanted to blame those rips on the dry cleaner," Carl said.

"You know I would never do that," she said. "You just don't like being wrong. You should work on that. I saw a segment on a TV talk show that said people who have trouble admitting when they're wrong often have trouble in general expressing themselves."

Before this conversation could veer any further off track, Dani returned to the main topic. "So after she made her romantic suggestion, how did your life change?"

Carl cleared his throat. Then he cleared his throat again. It was obvious he was uncomfortable. Finally, he said, "I met a young lady and fell in love."

When he didn't elaborate, Dani asked, "And then what happened?"

"I was so much in love, I lost focus on my business and it's now hovering on the brink of bankruptcy," he said. "Before Freda made that curse, my business was fine."

"You shouldn't have paid so much attention to that woman. She wasn't what I meant." Freda leaned back and folded her hands on the table. "Anyone would have known I didn't mean her."

Dani was amazed at how calm her grandmother was. Maybe it was because she and Carl were old friends. Dani got the distinct impression that Freda didn't truly believe Carl would actually file a lawsuit.

But Dani wasn't counting on their friendship to make it through this. She'd seen too many long-term relationships destroyed over less. When people got angry, they often lost sight of what mattered.

And Carl was good and mad. If his face got any redder, she was going to suggest they dial 911.

"You know Mrs. Karlinski can't give you the amount of money you're asking for," Dani said. "She doesn't have it, nor does she have any insurance that would cover such an expense. You also must realize that if you focus on your business and keep regular hours, you should be able to rebuild. So what is it that you want?"

Roger had been watching the whole process silently, but now he opened his notebook. "Mr. Whitley feels actions such as those you've suggested won't be enough. He wants to restart his business and has decided fifty thousand should let him rebuild. I understand Mrs. Karlinski has life insurance from her late husband and that since she lives with her son, her expenses are minimal. That amount shouldn't cause her any hardship."

Dani stared at him. Roger had to be kidding. Fifty thousand? For making one romantic suggestion?

Before she could say a word, Freda shook her head. "No. I will not do it. I was trying to make you happy, you old fool."

Then she stood and looked at Dani. "I'm done here. If he wants to file a lawsuit, then he can file a lawsuit. I'll fight him in court."

Without waiting for either Dani or Travis, Freda headed out the door. Dani looked at Travis, who had already stood.

"Can you go catch up with Freda? I'll be with you in a second."

Travis nodded. "Sure."

After Travis had left, Dani looked at Roger and Carl. "You know she's not going to be able to pay what you're asking. Although my father has money, Freda doesn't. She didn't receive much in insurance.

I think you'll need to consider how this case will sound if we do go to court. Do you really think you can convince anyone that Freda has magical powers and was able to make you do something you didn't want to do?" She gave both men a pitying look. "Seriously, who is going to believe that a sweet old lady can make people fall in love by placing spells on them?"

With that, Dani left, more than a little upset with Carl Whitley. He couldn't seriously expect her grandmother to pay such a ridiculous amount. Travis had uncovered a lot of things about Mr. Carl Whitley and how much he had ignored his business. Dani would use that information if she had to.

And one thing she knew for certain, her grandmother wouldn't change her mind. Even though she and Carl used to be friends, they weren't anymore, and Freda wasn't about to give him any money.

And no one was more stubborn than Freda Karlinski.

TRAVIS FOLLOWED Dani up the stairs to her apartment, barely resisting the urge to point out how stuffy the place was. Sure, it was elegant, but everything from the lobby with its oh-so-polite security guard to the staircase with its plush carpeting to the hallways with their subdued lighting and classy potted plants screamed Do Not Touch.

When they'd been here earlier, he'd gotten a phone call from Elvin so he'd waited in the car while she'd gone upstairs to change her clothes. He hadn't had a chance to see her place, but now that he was here, he could only hope her apartment was more relaxed than the common areas. This place was perfect for a stuffed shirt but that was the last thing Dani was.

"How long have you lived here?" Travis asked as they reached the second floor and headed down the hallway.

"Three years. It's a very discriminating building. I had to jump through a lot of hoops to get accepted," she told him.

"Ah. Well that explains why I don't live here," he said dryly.

Dani laughed. "Okay, it's…reserved. But at the time I rented here, I thought having this address would help my career."

"Did it?"

"No," she sighed. "Or maybe it would have if I'd ever had a chance to have parties here and show it off. But I'm so busy I don't have time to do things like have clients or people from work over."

They stopped at an impressive double door. Man, this place was nothing like his. Next to the door was a plant that was as fancy and elegant as the rest of the furnishings.

"Is this thing real?" He touched the shiny, somewhat spiky leaves.

Dani nudged him. "Yes, of course it's real. It's just very—"

"Reserved?"

She touched the plant lovingly. "Hey, I like this plant. We've been friends for the whole time I've lived here." After a second, she added, "I know it's silly, but I'm going to miss it."

Travis looked at the plant. What he was going to miss was Dani. Watching what had happened between Freda and Carl and their friendship, he realized that whatever sort of relationship he had with Dani would end once she moved. Time and distance didn't make things better. They'd both move on with their lives and the last few days would fade in their memories.

She quickly unlocked her front door and then led the way inside. Everything was in boxes and ready for the movers.

"Wow, it looks different from when I was here this morning." She wandered farther into the apartment, looking over the work the packers had done during the day.

Travis felt as though he'd taken a sucker punch to the gut. Seeing the evidence of her upcoming move only reinforced the reality of what was happening. Sadness engulfed him.

He'd never felt this way before, and it caught him off guard. He shouldn't be this unsettled about her departure. Sure, when some of his relationships had ended in the past, he'd felt a little sad, but nothing like this. Nothing like this empty, hollow feeling that was hitting him full-force.

This didn't make any sense. He was the last guy to want a long-term relationship. Settling down just wasn't his thing. Still, he'd like to spend more time with Dani. What they'd shared this last week had been terrific.

But what could he do? He couldn't ask her to stay. This job was something she'd worked toward for years. And he couldn't leave Chicago. He had the agency and his commitment to Max to consider.

"It's funny, but this new job is all I've thought about for the longest time." She sighed. "Actually, I've been working for this job for years. Even when I was in high school, I'd sit and talk with my father about making partner at a prestigious law firm someday."

"Did you and your dad talk a lot?" Travis asked, picking up on something in her tone. He'd never met Dani's father, but he definitely got the feeling the man wasn't exactly a loving, doting paternal figure.

Dani shook her head. "Not really. Mostly just about me making partner. My father was and still is focused on success. I actually think it's his hobby."

Travis was getting the picture very clearly. "So is this new job about him or about you?"

With an empty-sounding laugh, Dani said, "Don't try to psychoanalyze me, Travis. Sure my father shared his interest in success with me, but now it's my interest, too. I've worked many years and lots of long hours to get where I am today. Everything I've done in the past few years has been to achieve this goal."

"Hence the apartment in the reserved building," he said dryly.

She nodded slowly. "Yes."

Although it might not be smart, he asked the question he'd been dying to ask for a long time. "Do you ever have fun?"

Dani seemed surprised by his question. "Of course I have fun. This last week has been a lot of fun."

"But before that? Did you have fun? Ever take time off to relax?"

For several long seconds, she just looked at him. Then she finally shrugged. "Okay, maybe I don't have fun in the way we've had fun this last week. But I've enjoyed my life. I've enjoyed becoming a success."

Enjoyed. In Travis's opinion that wasn't the same as fun.

He glanced around at the neatly packed boxes. "So, any regrets now that you're moving?"

The look she gave him tugged at his heart. It was sweet and sad and made him regret not keeping in touch with her over the years. They'd been friends, and they should have remained friends.

"I regret not having more time to spend with you," she said.

"Yeah, me, too," he admitted, walking over to stand in front of her. "Watching Freda and Carl fight today made me realize how easy it is to lose a friendship."

He reached out and touched the side of her face, letting his fingers caress her soft skin. "I hate to think about us losing our friendship."

She smiled. "Sure it's not just the benefits you'll miss?"

"You'd think it would be, wouldn't you?" He smiled at her. "But that's not what I'll miss most. I'm going to miss hanging around with you, talking and laughing and having fun with you," he admitted.

"It has been a lot of fun," she said, her gaze locked with his. "I've never really felt this way about someone. You and I laugh and argue and talk. We always seem to understand each other even though we might not always agree. Plus we have amazing sex."

Yeah, what they had was unusual. Travis had never been as comfortable around a woman as he was around Dani. He slipped one arm around her waist and nodded toward the boxes.

"This is depressing. Why don't we grab your clothes and head back to my place? You're not leaving for two more days. I'd like to enjoy that time together."

He expected her to tease him about wanting more of the benefits, but she didn't. Apparently, she felt as sad as he did. Instead, she gathered up the clothes and personal items she hadn't had the movers pack and then joined him in the living room again.

"All set," she said when she was next to him. "Let's go have some fun."

Travis grinned, suddenly realizing what he could do for Dani. He might not be able to turn this relationship into something long-term, but he could make the remaining time they had together something she'd remember for the rest of her life.

He gave her a deep, long kiss, and then with a wink, promised, "Lady, you've come to the right guy if you're looking for fun."

11

DANI WANDERED around Travis's apartment, unable to help noticing how different it was from her place. Oh, sure, he didn't have everything packed up, which was the obvious difference.

But his apartment was also a place where someone actually lived. The chairs and sofa had been picked for comfort, not to impress. The room's colors were vivid and vibrant and full of life, with lots of blues and greens and not a pale beige in sight.

Funny, but when she'd been here before, she hadn't noticed how much style the place had. Of course, that oversight was probably due to her being so busy. She hadn't had time to notice his décor; she'd been too focused on Travis.

"Did you decorate this apartment yourself?" Dani asked once Travis had set down the bag of groceries they'd bought on the way over.

Travis looked around, his hands on his hips. "Yeah, I know it needs work, but it was the best I could do. I'm not really into decorating."

Dani laughed. "You goof. I'm saying I like it, not

that I hate it. Actually, I'm impressed. It's very comfortable and cozy. You did a great job."

With a twinkle in his eyes, he said, "You won't say that once you find out *how* I managed to decorate it." He started putting away the groceries in the kitchen, which was separated from the living room by a counter. Three stools were on the living room side of the counter, so Dani sat on one and watched him work.

When he finished, she said, "Okay, spill. What deep, dark decorating secret do you have? Do you have a burning desire to be a decorator?"

He laughed. "Not even close."

Dani pretended to think. "Oh, I know. I bet an old girlfriend did this for you. Or better yet, are you like Louise and you saw a show on TV that inspired you?"

Travis shook his head, a smile on his face. "Hey, I'm not completely helpless. You know we guys are good at a lot more than just sports and lifting heavy objects."

With a dip of her head, Dani recanted. "I stand corrected. So you came up with this decorating scheme all on your own."

After a second, Travis chuckled. "Okay, I'll fess up. I went into a furniture store and they had all these rooms already designed. They had a living room—" he nodded toward his living room "—dining room, bedroom and guest bedroom."

"Oh, so that's how you did it."

He nodded. "Afraid so. I just walked through the showroom and bought each room. Then I painted the rooms the same way they'd painted them. I think the whole thing lost a little in translation, but it was quick and easy and it worked."

Dani glanced around the living room and the dining room. Now that she considered them, the rooms did have a sort of professional look.

"Did you buy the accessories as well as the furniture?" she asked, noticing the knickknacks scattered around. Travis didn't strike her as a knickknack kind of guy.

Travis leaned across the counter separating them and kissed her. "Why so many questions about my apartment?"

"Because I'm curious about you," she admitted. "We haven't spoken in years, and this past week, we've been so busy with the case and..." She waved one hand between them. "With other things, that I haven't had a chance to really catch up with your life."

Travis grabbed something from the freezer, and then walked around to her side of the counter. Sitting on the stool next to hers, he handed her an ice cream sandwich.

"For energy," he said with a laugh. "You'll probably need it later."

Knowing that if she had any say in the matter, she definitely would need that energy before the night was over, Dani took the ice cream.

"So when you moved into this place you went to a store and bought what they had on display," she said, unwrapping her ice cream and picking up the conversation where they'd left off.

Travis nudged her with his knees. "You know Max and I grew up all over the world. Since Dad was in the army, we moved constantly. When I rented this apartment, I knew I was staying put, so I wanted it to look nice. I didn't have a clue how to do it, and I figured whoever designed those layouts in the store knew more than I did."

"The place looks great," she said.

With a self-deprecating laugh, he said, "Well, left to my own limited devices, the apartment would have been a disaster, and I wasn't going to hire a decorator. So I came up with my own solution."

"I like your solution," she said, taking a bite of her ice cream sandwich. "I paid a decorator a fortune to do my apartment, and it turned out white and beige and filled with glass. Nothing was comfortable, and even though I'll miss a lot of things in Chicago, that won't be one of them."

"Will you hire a decorator for your New York apartment?" he asked.

"Probably," she admitted, although she hadn't considered that far ahead yet. "But first I have to find a place to live."

"Didn't you go to New York for interviews? I would have thought you would have found a place then."

She finished her ice cream and neatly folded the wrapper into a small square. Then she looked at him. "Yes, but I never felt like searching for a place. When I was there, I was busy with meetings. And once the meetings ended, I had to get back to

Chicago, so I figured I'd find a place after I moved."

"It doesn't bother you moving there without a place to live?"

Dani opened her mouth to tell him the same story she always told everyone when they asked her questions like this, but then she changed her mind. She decided to tell Travis the truth.

"The main reason I didn't find a place was because I thought that if I looked for an apartment, it would jinx the job offer."

The humor lurking in his eyes told her he found this funny. "You believe in jinxes?"

She started to stand, but he turned on his bar stool to block her. With a sigh, she said, "I know what you're thinking."

"You do, do you?"

"Yes, you're thinking I'm as loony as my grandmother. She believes she can go around putting curses on people and I believe I can jinx events. We're both nuts."

He stood, which placed him directly in front of her. "You're not nuts," he said. "The world is filled with many confusing and mysterious things."

Dani would have laughed at this, except he started sliding one hand up under her skirt, and her mind became a little preoccupied.

"Hmm," was the best she could do as he caressed her knee, his fingers slowly tracing tantalizing patterns on her skin.

"Take cowlicks," he said. "What's the point of them? Why do some people have them and others don't? And why didn't society come up with a better name for them?"

His hand moved up a couple more inches, and Dani gave him a knowing smile. "Travis Walker, are you trying to seduce me?"

He grinned. "Who said anything about *trying*?"

Dani leaned back against the counter. "In that case, continue."

Travis moved closer and nibbled lightly on her earlobe while his fingers caressed the sensitive skin of her thigh. She wanted so very much for his hand to shift, to move just a tiny bit to the right, so he could help her satisfy the craving he was creating inside her.

"You're not crazy at all," he murmured as he dropped kisses down her neck. "Just confused. About life. Like the rest of us."

Dani would have agreed with him, but he finally shifted his hand, and she sighed.

"Travis," she breathed, turning her head so she could kiss him. At the same second that she slipped her tongue inside his mouth, he slipped his fingers under her panties.

Dani wrapped her arms around his neck, kissing him deeply while his talented fingers explored her. The tension building within her was both sweet and tormenting. As he dipped a finger inside her, he continued to kiss her.

Then he set up a rhythm that made her squirm with pleasure.

"Travis," she murmured, burying her head in his shoulder as the pressure within her built.

"Soon," he assured her. "Enjoy it, Gypsy."

And she did. She let the sensations overtake her, moving her closer and closer to the brink. Finally, Travis picked up the speed, pushing her to the release she so desperately craved.

Afterward, Dani kissed him again. Softly, slowly. "That was nice."

His smile was tender and tugged at her heart. "Glad you liked it."

She tipped her head and studied his face. He was so sexy and sweet and kind and funny...and wonderful. Travis had always been a great guy, but now she realized he was unlike any man she'd ever known. She felt cherished when she was with him, felt complete.

Dani blinked. Then blinked again. This couldn't be happening. Not to her. Not now.

But it was, and she now knew with absolute certainty that despite her best efforts, she was falling in love with Travis.

The realization was so strong and so sudden that she literally jumped away from him.

"What's wrong?" he asked, obviously surprised.

She knew his concern was genuine. Of course it was. Travis Walker was a great guy. A nice guy who cared about other people and who would naturally care that something had upset her.

No wonder she'd fallen for him. She should have realized from the start that he was too nice a guy to get involved with.

Needing space, Dani moved to the far side of the living room. She looked at him, knowing the smart thing to do would be to lie and not tell him what she'd discovered. Telling him would only upset them both, and there was nothing to be gained by that. She was moving in two days. Then it would be over.

There was no reason for Travis to know what she was feeling.

"Dani, what's wrong?" He took a step toward her, but stopped when she held up one hand.

"I…" She cleared her throat and tried again. "I can't do this."

Obviously confused, he asked, "Can't do what?"

"I can't feel this way." She hadn't meant to say that, so she slammed her mouth shut before she said any more. What was she supposed to do now? She ran one hand through her hair. Of all the stupid things to do, why would she fall for him? She had plans, plans that didn't and couldn't include him. She was a smart woman. Too smart to do something this dumb.

"Dani, I don't understand. Talk to me." Travis took another step toward her. "Whatever's wrong, we can sort it out together."

She looked at him, and again love rushed through her. She supposed most people would be thrilled to realize they were in love. Most people wouldn't act as though they'd just discovered a rattlesnake in their car.

She knew Travis deserved an explanation, so Dani tried to come up with one. There had to be something she could say that he'd buy. Something that would keep him from realizing what had really happened.

She took a deep breath and tried to lie, but instead blurted, "This wasn't supposed to happen."

"What wasn't?"

"I know we made certain promises to each other and to ourselves when we started this thing between us," she said, unable to lie to him. She watched his reaction closely. So far, he just seemed confused.

"Okay. So do you want to stop, is that what you're saying? Do you think we should stop now rather than wait until you move?" The tense tone of his voice told her what he was feeling. He didn't want things to end.

"No. Yes." She sighed. "I don't know. I just know I've done something so incredibly stupid I can't believe it."

Travis shook his head. "Not you. You would never do something stupid."

"But I did," she said with a humorless laugh. "I know I promised I wouldn't, but I think I'm falling in love with you."

Travis stood perfectly still, his expression unreadable. Dani had no idea what he was thinking, no idea what he was feeling, and she found herself holding her breath while she waited for his reaction.

"I know. I can't believe I've done this," she said after a few seconds when he still hadn't said a word.

She sat on his sofa, feeling like a complete idiot. She was a woman in control of her emotions. How had she let this happen?

She glanced at Travis and said, "You know, actually this is your fault."

Travis walked over and sat next to her on the couch. "My fault? How is your falling for me my fault?"

"You're the one who is so terrific that I can't resist you," she said dryly. "You should work on that."

"Ah, well in that case, the fact that I'm falling for you is your fault," he said softly. "You're so terrific I couldn't help *my*self."

Dani stared at him. Part of her was thrilled to hear him say he felt the same way, but the other part of her, the rational part, realized just how terrible this situation was.

"Oh no," she said. "We can't both have been that stupid. We promised. We agreed. We both understood the rules going in."

After draping one arm around her shoulders and giving her a hug, Travis said, "Well at least we're stupid together."

"But we both agreed up front that we wouldn't fall for each other. We were clear about that. Trav, Louise manages to do this without any problems. Why couldn't we?"

He shrugged. "I don't know."

"I'm leaving in two days, and I can't change my plans. I've accepted that job, and they'll notice if I don't show up." She leaned back against him, enjoying the warmth and comfort of being near him while at the same time knowing that moments like this only made things worse. "I beat out fifteen candidates. I can't just say thanks but I've changed my mind. I have my career to think of."

He nodded. "I know. And I wouldn't want you to give up this opportunity."

"This is terrible," she said.

"The only good thing is that at least we're admitting how we feel." Travis dropped a kiss on her forehead. "And I do mean it. I've never felt this way about anyone. It's about more than just great sex—"

Dani nodded solemnly. "Terrific sex."

"Fantastic sex."

With a laugh, Dani said, "Okay, fantastic sex. But it's more than that. It's about how comfortable I feel around you."

"Yeah, it is." He gathered her closer. "I know it sounds stupid, but it feels right."

That was exactly how it felt to Dani, too. It felt right, like they were meant to be together. But she also knew that love often faded, and just because she and Travis had strong feelings for each other now, was it enough to risk what she'd worked her entire life for?

"I don't know what to do," she admitted.

"Do you think there's any way we can make this work long-distance? I know it wouldn't be easy, with you in New York and me here, but we can try."

Dani wanted to say yes, that they should try. But in her heart she knew that wouldn't work. She was going to be so busy when she got to New York she'd be lucky if she had time to breathe, let alone continue a relationship.

No, the smart thing to do was to make a clean break of things now to avoid the complications that would happen once she moved. But the thought of breaking things off with Travis made pain lodge deep and sharp within her chest.

"How about we avoid any decisions at least for tonight," she suggested, knowing she was being a coward by putting off the discussion, but unable to help herself. She wanted every moment she could have with him, and she really couldn't think straight just now. Realizing that she was falling for him—along with learning he was falling for her—was more than she could deal with.

"Okay," he said. "We'll think about it and see what we can come up with."

"Yes, and maybe in the morning things will look clearer."

Although she knew they probably wouldn't, she was happy when Travis agreed to sleep on it. And who knew? Maybe by morning they would be able to think of another solution.

"Works for me." He leaned over and gave her a long, lingering kiss. "But I can guarantee you, I won't feel any differently about you tomorrow than I do tonight."

"But maybe we'll come up with some better ideas

on how to handle what we're feeling," she pointed out. "Maybe by morning, the solution will be right in front of us."

He gave her a dubious look, then said, "Maybe. In the meantime, why don't I feed you dinner? Then, after that we can—"

"Top things off with that fantastic sex we discussed earlier?"

Travis chuckled. "Sounds like a plan to me."

TRAVIS ROLLED OVER and glanced at the clock on the nightstand. A little after three in the morning. Man, he needed to stop thinking about Dani and fall asleep. At this rate, he'd be dead on his feet in the morning.

The problem was, he couldn't get his brain to shut off. All he could focus on was the knowledge that not only was he falling for Dani, but that she was falling for him, too.

On one hand, he was happy she felt what he did. They were good together and they both knew it. But on the other hand, getting seriously involved was the last thing either of them wanted or needed to do at the moment. They had too many important things happening right now, things they couldn't risk on the chance that what they were feeling would last.

He hadn't a clue what was the right thing to do, not only for himself, but also for Dani. He knew he couldn't ask her to stay here in Chicago with him any more than she could ask him to go to New York with her. Max and the agency depended on him. He couldn't leave.

And if they tried to make things work long-distance, would they instead kill what was growing between them?

He sighed and continued to stare at the ceiling. Maybe this was why he'd never fallen in love before—it was complicated and messy. Why would people want to put themselves through this?

But deep inside, he knew that wasn't why he hadn't fallen in love before. The bottom line was, he'd never fallen because he'd never met anyone like Dani. She was truly one of a kind. He'd known it years ago when they'd been friends, and he knew it now.

He also knew he'd never meet another woman like her.

The faint ringing of a phone startled him. Out of habit, he grabbed for the phone on the bedside table, but quickly realized the noise was coming from Dani's purse. It had to be her cell phone ringing.

He turned on the light by the bed and then walked across the room to get her purse. When he returned to the bed, Travis lightly shook her. "Dani, your phone is ringing."

One thing he'd learned about Dani the last few nights was she didn't wake up easily. She slept so soundly that it took several seconds to get her even to acknowledge he'd spoken to her. When she finally opened her eyes, she groaned when Travis handed her the purse.

"Who would call me in the middle of the night?" she asked as she dug for the phone. The ringing had stopped by the time she found it. After a couple of seconds, a short beep let her know there was a message.

Still muttering, she checked to see the number of the caller.

"It's from my parents' house," she said, tension in her voice, obviously awake now.

Travis had a bad feeling about this. People didn't call in the middle of the night for no reason, and in his experience, they only called when the news was urgent and usually not good.

As Dani listened to the message that had been left, her face grew pale.

"She's missing," Dani told him.

"Who's missing?"

"My grandmother," Dani replied. "My father said she's disappeared."

Travis stood and started getting dressed while Dani returned the phone call from her father. From what he could gather from Dani's side of the conversation, Freda had called a cab about six this evening and then left without telling anyone where she was going.

By the time Dani hung up, Travis was completely dressed and ready to go when she was. When he looked at her, she had tears in her eyes.

"I won't be able to stand it if something happens to her," Dani said softly.

Travis felt as if a sword had pierced his chest. He sat next to her on the bed and wrapped his arms around her. As he held her close, he said, "Nothing will happen to her. We'll find her."

"I hope so. Freda does crazy things. She doesn't understand that not everyone in the world is good," Dani said, wiping her tears. "Where could she have gone that she's not home yet?"

"I don't know," Travis admitted. "But let's go over to your parents' house and see what we can do to help find her. And we will find her. Don't worry."

As Dani got dressed, Travis made calls to the local hospitals just to make certain that Freda hadn't been in an accident. He breathed a sigh of relief when he determined she wasn't at any of them.

"So far, so good," he told Dani when she was ready to go. "Since she's not in any of the hospitals, that means she's probably okay."

Dani nodded, but as they headed toward the parking garage, he could tell she didn't really believe him. To make her feel better, he reached down and took one of her hands in his.

"It will be okay," he assured her. "Everything is going to be okay."

"I hope you're right," she whispered.

Yeah, so did he.

12

On the way to her parents' house, Dani was so upset she could barely talk. Fortunately, Travis was being sweet, as always, but she knew her parents would be impossible to deal with. Repeatedly, on the phone, her father had mentioned how Freda was messing up the good night's sleep he needed so he could function the next day.

The man was amazing. His own mother was missing and all he could talk about was how it was going to impact his job.

Unbelievable.

"What exactly happened?" Travis asked as he exited the interstate. "Why did she leave?"

"Apparently, my father and grandmother got into a fight about the potential lawsuit. My father thinks she should just pay Carl what he wants and then sweep the whole thing under the carpet." Dani sighed, knowing her father would never understand his own mother. If he understood her, he would never have suggested such a thing.

"Naturally she refused," Travis said.

"Exactly. She refused then went to her room. My father said he didn't see her for a couple of hours, and the next thing he noticed was a cab pulling up in front of the house. Before he could stop her, she left."

Even saying that made Dani's chest tighten. Her grandmother was a smart lady, but she was also way too trusting. What if something terrible had happened to her?

"When she left, did she take anything with her?" Travis asked.

"Like what?"

"A suitcase, clothes, that sort of thing."

"I don't know. I didn't think to ask my father and he didn't mention it," she admitted. Then she asked, "Where do you think she went?"

"Maybe to a friend's house," he said. "Or to a hotel to get away for a while and let the air clear."

Dani considered his suggestions, but she couldn't think of any friends that Freda had who would be close enough to welcome her to stay over. A hotel seemed the most likely possibility.

"I'm sorry about this," Dani told Travis as he pulled into the driveway of her parents' house.

"First, you have nothing to be sorry about. Second, all that matters is that Freda's okay," he told her.

Dani couldn't resist asking, "Aren't you upset that you're being dragged over here in the middle of the night because of my grandmother?"

Travis parked the car, and then turned to look at her. "No, why would I be? All that matters is that your grandmother is okay. I really like Freda. I care about her and want her safe just like you do."

Love washed through Dani. How could she not love this man? He was so caring and sweet that, as she'd told him earlier, she'd had no choice but to fall in love with him. Who wouldn't love him?

Leaning over, she kissed him soundly. "You are the most wonderful man in the world."

Travis chuckled. "You've met them all, have you?"

"I've met enough," she assured him. She glanced at her parents' house. She'd expected all the lights to be on, but as usual, there was no sign that a crisis was happening inside. A few discreet lights shone from various rooms, but that was all. How typical.

Pushing open her car door, she climbed out, and then walked up the front stairs with Travis.

"Do you have a key?" he asked.

Dani shook her head. "No, when I moved out and got my own place, my father asked for my key back since I no longer lived here."

Because Travis stood under one of the lanterns mounted on either side of the door, she could clearly see his stunned expression. "Really? But you're his daughter. Was he upset that you were moving out? Is that why he asked for the key back?"

"No. He actually wanted me to move out. He's a man who doesn't like loose ends, and he felt me having a key was a loose end," she explained. At the time, it had upset her that he'd made such a big deal about the key, but over the years, she'd forgotten about it so it no longer bothered her.

But apparently it bothered Travis. He pulled his keyring out of his pocket and yanked a key off it. "Here. Have a key to my apartment. I want you to know how special you are to me."

Dani appreciated the gesture and understood why he was doing it, but she didn't feel right about taking his key—especially under the circumstances and especially since it was his only key.

"I don't think I should—"

"Take it."

Since he seemed adamant, she took it.

"I'm giving this back to you when we leave here," she told him, slipping the key inside her purse. "Just so you know."

"We'll talk about it later," was all he said. Then he reached out and rang the doorbell.

It took almost a minute before the wide door opened. When it did, her father stood on the threshold, already dressed for the day in a subdued gray suit.

"Can you believe your grandmother did this? I have several important meetings today. I needed to get a good night's sleep. I can't do this right now," he said.

He walked toward the living room, talking as he went and not bothering to see if they were following. Dani stared after him. How could he be the son of someone as full of life and as interested in other people as Freda was? She'd never met her grandfather, he'd died long before she was born, but Dani could only assume her father took after him.

Dani walked inside the house, but when she realized Travis wasn't with her, she glanced back at him.

"What's wrong?" she asked.

He smiled and looked almost happy. What did he have to be smiling about?

"I have an idea," he said. "Detective's instinct. I'll be back in a few minutes."

She took a step toward him, not wanting him to leave. "Where are you going?"

He just kept smiling. "I'll tell you when I get back. Don't worry."

Then, without further explanation, he left, shutting the front door behind him. Dani stared at the closed door. What idea? What was he doing?

And why'd he have to leave her here alone with her parents? With a sigh, she reluctantly headed toward the living room to talk to them. Maybe she could get some information from them that would help find Freda.

"What took you so long to get in here?" her father asked impatiently when she entered the room. "And where's that man? Is he the detective your grandmother talks incessantly about?"

Dani glanced at her mother. Like her father, she was immaculately dressed for the day. Didn't these people realize it was the middle of the night?

"Yes, that's Travis Walker. I went to high school with him, remember?" She sat on the sofa next to her mother, who frowned at her.

"You brought that man here? Why?" her mother asked. "I think he's just soaking you for money, Danielle."

"And where is he?" Her father paced in front of the fireplace at the far end of the room. "If you're paying him, shouldn't he be doing something to earn his money?"

"He had an idea so he's gone to check on it," she explained.

"I don't like him," her father announced. "You should have hired someone more professional, someone who has been in the business a much longer time. That young man strikes me as incompetent."

Dani started to tell her father he didn't know a thing about Travis and his skill as a detective, but she kept her mouth shut, as she always did when her father upset her.

"You have to watch out for people like that, Danielle," her father said. "They may seem like they're doing a good job, but that's only because they're good at hiding their incompetence."

Okay, that was it. No matter how hard she tried to keep her mouth shut, it refused to stay that way.

"Travis is not incompetent. He's an excellent detective and an even better person and I love him," she blurted out, surprising even herself.

"You *what?*" Her mother stared at her as if she'd said she could fly by flapping her arms.

Frankly, Dani hadn't a clue why she had told her parents she was in love with Travis, but now that she had, she wasn't sorry. She was lucky to have such a great person to love, even if it probably wouldn't work out.

"I'm in love with him," she repeated, liking the way those words sounded as they came out of her mouth. "He's a terrific man."

"This is ridiculous," her father said. "You can't be in love with anyone right now. You have your job to consider. A man like that would be baggage to your career. He could destroy everything you've worked for. You can't let silly emotions get in your way."

"This is inappropriate," her mother said, smoothing the skirt of her dress. "You have responsibilities and plans, Danielle. I thought you were too smart to let a pretty face distract you."

Although Dani hadn't expected them to congratulate her on being in love, she still was disappointed that they were so negative.

"Travis is a lot more than a pretty face, and he's not interfering with my new job. In fact, we've both admitted that our relationship probably won't work because he needs to stay in Chicago with the detective agency and I need to be in New York."

"I'm glad to hear you're being sensible about this," her father said. Then he glanced at his watch. "How much longer is your grandmother going to keep this up? I need to be at work in three hours."

Again, Dani tried to keep her mouth closed and hold in the words she knew she shouldn't say, and again the words jumped out.

"What is wrong with you two? Nana Freda could be lost or hurt and all you care about is your schedules. Don't you love anyone or anything? Did you ever truly love each other?"

When they stared at her blankly, Dani asked, "Did you ever really love me?"

"You're being ridiculous," her mother said. "You know how we feel about you."

But she didn't.

Finally, when neither of them made the least effort to tell her that they loved her, she decided the sooner she got out of this room, the better. Who knew what she'd blurt out next?

Standing, she said, "I'm going to try calling hotels. Maybe we can find Freda before something bad happens to her."

"Danielle, don't walk out on us," her father said in the booming voice he used with the people who worked for him.

When she'd been growing up, Dani had jumped through hoops to keep him from ever using that voice with her. But she wasn't a little girl anymore, and she was tired of trying to please parents who realistically would probably never be happy with anything she did.

So instead of stopping, she kept walking, heading toward the study. She had something more important to do tonight than fight with her parents.

She had to find her grandmother.

TRAVIS PULLED UP in front of the small suburban house and smiled. He'd known all along his instincts as a detective were good, but tonight, he was proving it. Every light in the house was on, and even with the windows closed, Travis could hear music playing from inside.

He climbed out of his car and walked to the front door. He'd expected them to be playing Big Band or maybe Elvis, but instead, they were playing the Rolling Stones. Really loudly.

"I guess age really is relative," he said to himself as he rang the doorbell.

He'd barely had time to pull his hand back when the door flew open and Freda grinned at him. "I won't bother to ask how you found me since it's your job to find things. Dani said you were good, and you are."

"Hello, Freda," he said. "I guess you know that everyone is worried about you."

She waved one finger in front of him. "Tsk, tsk, Travis, don't lie. The only one worried about me is Dani. My son has never worried about anything but his job in his entire life. If I hadn't given birth to him, I would swear he wasn't mine."

"You need to go home," Travis told her. He glanced down the hallway. "Hello, Carl."

Carl moved forward slowly, a sheepish smile on his face. "How did you know she was here?"

"It's his job to find things," Freda said. "And he's good at it."

"So he knows about us?" Carl shoved his glasses farther up on his nose.

Travis looked from one to the other, taking in their disheveled clothing, and then held back a smile.

"I had a hunch about you two," he said, which hadn't exactly been true. He'd known they were friends and had thought Freda had probably gone to Carl's to try to work this problem out between the two of them.

What he hadn't realized was that they were much more than friends.

"We're in love, so I don't want any comments," Freda said, snagging her purse. "Come on, Carl. Let's go see my son and tell him."

Carl trailed after her, a goofy smile on his face. "Isn't she wonderful?"

Travis nodded as he watched Freda head for the car. "Yep, she's wonderful."

"This time I'm not letting her slip away," Carl said as he locked the front door behind them.

"This time?"

"I spent years asking Freda out, but she always said she'd already been in love once in her life and that was all a person got. Every time she said that, I got madder and madder, until finally we had the fight that led to the curse. But tonight, I made her understand that I'm serious. I love her and want her in my life, and I'll do whatever it takes to make that happen."

With that, Carl headed toward the car, leaving Travis trailing after him. Although Travis had known he'd find Freda at Carl's, he hadn't expected the rest.

Man, wait until Dani heard this.

Thinking of Dani, he pulled out his cell phone and had started to call her when Freda said from the back seat, "Let them wait until we get there. I don't want to give my son time to work up an argument. Carl and I will fare better if we take him by surprise."

Travis clipped his phone back on his belt. "Okay. You're in charge."

Freda had Carl climb into the back seat with her and then she gave Travis a regal look. "Yes, I am."

WHEN DANI heard a car pull up in front of the house, she practically fell over her own feet getting to the door. She flung it open and then let out a cry of joy when she saw her grandmother.

"You had us scared to death," she told Freda as she wrapped her in a bear hug. "Don't ever do that again."

Freda patted her cheek. "I won't, sweetie, but I had to take care of something really important."

For the first time since the car had pulled up, Dani noticed Carl.

Dani blinked and looked at her grandmother. "You went to Carl's house?"

Without answering the question, her grandmother headed through the front door. "Come on. I need to tell your parents something."

Carl gave Dani a small smile and then caught up with Freda. When the older man slipped an arm around her grandmother's waist, Dani turned to stare at Travis.

"Am I missing something here?" she asked.

He came over and stood next to her. "Apparently, we all were missing something, including your grandmother. She didn't realize quite how much Carl loved her."

Dani's mouth dropped open. "You're kidding?"

"Not a bit," he assured her as they walked toward the living room. "They were like a couple of rowdy teenagers in my back seat the whole way over here."

"Way to go, Nana."

When they entered the living room, Freda was holding court. She pointed directly at her son and said, "I'm going to live with Carl, so it doesn't really matter how you feel about it. We're in love."

"I'll tell you how I feel," her father yelled. "I forbid it."

Freda laughed. "You can't forbid me from doing something. I'm your mother."

Dani watched as her father grappled with that statement. In a way, she felt sorry for him. He wasn't used to people standing up to him, and now both she and her grandmother had done it on the same day— or in the same night.

Still, he needed to let people make their own choices and the sooner he learned that, the better. He'd gotten his way in life for far too long.

"I don't know what's wrong with the world," her

mother said. "First Danielle, and now you, Freda. Both of you are being very rude."

Freda glanced at Dani. "First Danielle what? What sort of announcement did you make, Dani?"

Dani glanced at Travis, who raised one eyebrow. Before she could answer her grandmother, her mother said, "Just like you, she's in love with someone who is completely wrong for her. I think both of you are crazy."

Dani looked at Travis. "Sorry. I didn't mean to tell them. It just slipped out."

"I'm glad," he said, leaning down and kissing her, right there in front of her parents. At first, Dani started to pull away, and then it hit her. Why shouldn't she kiss Travis? She was in love with him.

So she kissed him back, hard, and when they finally ended the kiss, her grandmother laughed.

"Good for you, Dani and Travis. I knew you two belonged together," she said.

Carl rolled his eyes. "Don't tell me you put a curse on them?"

Freda winked at her granddaughter. "I didn't have to. They fell in love all on their own." Then with a nudge to Carl, she added, "And they're romantic suggestions, not curses."

"It doesn't matter what all this nonsense is," her father boomed. "Danielle has a new career awaiting her, and she's not foolish enough to throw it away for something as ridiculous as love."

Dani started to answer, but Travis stopped her. "She shouldn't have to choose," he said. Then he looked at Dani, "I've given this a lot of thought, and I want to come to New York with you."

Dani stared at him. "But what about your job? What about the agency?"

"Max is a believer in love," Travis told her. "He'll understand, and he can run the agency fine without me. But I wouldn't be fine without you."

"Tell him yes," Freda said.

Dani looked at Travis, love overwhelming her. As much as she wanted to tell him yes, that he should come with her, she knew it was the wrong choice to make. She looked at her parents, who despite the problems between them were her family. Then she looked at her grandmother, a person who meant the world to her.

Finally, she looked at Travis.

"All that's in New York is a job," she said, her choice suddenly clear to her.

"And you," Travis said. "You'll be in New York, and I want to be where you are."

With a smile, Dani explained, "Then you'll want to live in Chicago because that's where I'll be."

"Dani, don't give up that great job because of me," Travis said, taking her hands in his. "You've worked years for this opportunity."

"Because I thought it would make me happy, but I know now it won't. It's just a job. I can land a great job here in Chicago," she said. "But the only thing that's going to truly make me happy is being with you and my family."

"Danielle, think about what you're doing," her father cautioned.

She looked at him and felt sorry for him. Obviously he'd never been in love the way she was.

"I am thinking about what I'm doing," she told him. "I'm doing what will make me happy."

"Are you sure about this?" Travis asked.

"Yes, I want to live here with you and with our families," she told him.

Travis grinned at her. "You sure?"

"Positive."

He kissed her again and then asked, "So how do you feel about marriage?"

Delighted, Dani told him, "I really, really like that idea."

"I can't believe this," her mother said walking over to stand next to her father. "Can you believe what she's doing?"

Her father frowned at her, but before he could say a word, Freda raised her right hand and pointed her index finger at them.

"Nana," Dani said in an effort to stop her grandmother, but she was too late.

"Love will fill your days," Freda said loudly.

Carl groaned. "Freda, I thought you agreed to stop doing that. People don't like it when you curse them. It makes them nervous."

Freda smiled. "I'm trying, but old habits die hard. And they are not curses."

Dani looked at her parents. Stunned. That was the

only way to describe their expressions. A couple of weeks ago she wouldn't have believed anything could change her parents. Now, thanks to her grandmother, she knew they were in for a big surprise.

And she was happy for them. Her parents needed love in their lives. As silly and irrational as it seemed, Dani was certain that due to Freda's romantic suggestion, her parents were about to experience the joys of love.

Smiling, she looked at Travis. "I love you."

"I love you, too, Gypsy," he said.

Dani had started to kiss him when she heard Freda say, "Love will be with you forever."

She and Travis both looked at her grandmother and realized she was talking to them.

"We already knew that," Travis told Freda. Then he kissed Dani.

Dani wrapped her arms around his neck and held him tightly.

Oh, yeah, they'd definitely already known that.

* * * * *

1

AH, NOTHING LIKE a little confrontation to start off a gorgeous April morning. A block away from her shop, Austin Body Art, Theresa Jacobs stopped and frowned at the half-dozen picketers milling around the tattoo parlor.

Keep Austin Clean one of their signs read. Take Back Sixth Street proclaimed another. Stamp Out Smut said a third. She had to hand it to them—these folks didn't give up easily. They'd been out there every day for the past two weeks.

Two of the group wore oversize white T-shirts with the words Vote Darryl "Clean" Carter For Austin City Council on them. Ah, yes, "Clean" Carter. Self-appointed protector of citizen morals and champion of a family-friendly Austin. Apparently he'd decided that running Theresa, and others like her, out of business would be the ideal way to win his campaign.

Clearly, Mr. Carter didn't realize how stubborn smut-sellers like her could be. She shifted her bag higher on her shoulder and tugged her leather halter top down a little lower. Cleavage exposed—

check. Belly-button ring showing—check. High-heeled boots, black fishnet hose, leather miniskirt—check. Big hair—check. Red, red lips—check. If Carter's minions expected sex, sin and sensation, she didn't want to disappoint them.

Sultry smile in place, she started walking toward the shop once more, moving in an exaggerated strut that had her hips swaying like a clock pendulum.

As they had each morning for the past two weeks, the protesters stopped and stared at her approach. "Good morning," she said, flashing a big smile as she inserted her key in the front door lock.

"Good morn—" one of the men started to return her greeting, but was cut off by an elbow in the ribs from the stern-faced woman at his side.

"We're having a special today, folks," Theresa said. "Half-priced piercings. I know you won't want to miss that."

"You ought to be ashamed of yourself." A tall woman with hair the color of apricots stepped forward. "What if you had a daughter who dressed and acted the way you do?"

Theresa lowered her sunglasses and looked the woman up and down. "I'd say she was having a lot more fun than someone who dressed and acted the way *you* do."

On this exit line, she entered the shop and punched in her alarm code. Another day of fun and excitement at Austin Body Art. If only the moral dictators out there realized how mundane most of her life and her clients really were. She might look like a wild woman, but lately an exciting evening for her was a cable movie and Lean Cuisine.

With this depressing thought she switched on the lights, booted up the computer and prepared to start the day. Before long the bells on the front door jangled. Theresa turned to greet the two men who entered.

It probably would be more appropriate to say the men made an entrance. The first one was a tall drink of water in scuffed boots, sharply creased Wranglers, a denim shirt and a straw hat tilted low on his forehead. He strode into the room like a marshal stepping into a saloon in an old Western. Broad-shouldered, narrow-waisted, with a strong chin and a slightly crooked nose, he was movie-star handsome. She blinked a few times to make sure he was even real, wishing he'd take off the hat so she could get a look at his eyes. Not that she was interested in the average cowboy, but she could appreciate a gorgeous man as much as the next girl. "What can I do for you, gentlemen?" she asked.

His companion, a short, bow-legged man in a Bull Riders Stay On Longer T-shirt, removed his hat and stared, open-mouthed, at the neckline of her halter top.

The taller man slapped his friend on the back of the head. "Put your eyes back in your skull and answer the lady."

His words broke the spell his initial appearance had put over her and for the first time she noticed the cast on his left forearm. The bright blue gauze wrapping made a sharp contrast to his deeply tanned skin.

He nodded to her and nudged his hat up enough for her to see his whiskey-colored eyes glinting with good humor.

To her astonishment, and utter mortification, she felt her heart flutter. She had to force back the smile she knew would have looked ridiculously goofy. Adonis here was no doubt used to women swooning at his feet, and she didn't intend to be one of them.

"I apologize for my friend. He's not used to associating with females other than cows and horses," Handsome Hank said.

"Shut your gob, Kyle." The shorter cowboy rubbed the back of his neck and focused his gaze somewhere over Theresa's left shoulder. "I'm interested in a tattoo."

"Then you came to the right place." With businesslike briskness, she plucked a clipboard from the rack by the counter and handed it to him. "Fill this out and we'll get started."

While he sat and began filling out the information and release form, she turned to his friend, Kyle. He was watching her, a speculative look in his eyes. The intensity of his gaze unnerved her. "Do you want a tattoo, too?"

The slow smile that formed on his lips would have knocked a lesser woman off her feet. As it was, Theresa took a step back and put one hand on the counter to steady herself.

"That's okay. Us naturally good-looking folks don't need any extra decoration." His gaze swept over the tiger etched on her shoulder, then shifted to the Celtic knot between her breasts. His smile broadened. "Though I have to say, you give me a whole new appreciation for your, um, art."

She laughed. "I'm sure you're a real art lover." She nodded to his cast. "What happened?"

He frowned at the injury. "Had a little trouble with an uncooperative bovine."

"Kyle has lousy luck with cattle and women." The shorter man, whose name turned out to be George, stood and handed the clipboard to Theresa.

"Don't mind him," Kyle said. "He's been tossed on his head by bulls one too many times."

"You're a bull rider?" Theresa scanned the release form. Everything looked okay.

"Yes, ma'am." George threw back his shoulders and puffed out his chest. "I'm in the top fifteen on the circuit right now."

She glanced at Kyle. "Are you a bull rider, too?"

He shook his head. "No, I have more sense."

"He's too tall to ride bulls," George said. "He's a calf roper." He glanced at the arm. "Or was."

"I can still whip you with one arm tied behind my back."

She somehow refrained from rolling her eyes at this typical male posturing. Honestly, was she supposed to be impressed? "Do you know what you want for your tat?" she asked George.

"I want a big lizard." He pointed to his forearm. "Right here."

"A lizard?"

"Yep. 'Cause that's my handle on the circuit. George 'the Lizard' Lizardi."

"Okay." She led him to a thick binder on a stand by the counter and flipped through it until she came to the reptile section. "You ought to find something here."

"George is a little nervous about needles," Kyle said.

Theresa nodded. "He'll be fine once we get started. For most people the anticipation of getting a tattoo is a lot more uncomfortable than the tat itself."

"What's your name?"

The question was a reasonable one, but it still caught her off guard. She started to ask him why he was interested, then thought better of it. He was a customer—or at least the buddy of a customer—so she ought to be polite. "Theresa Jacobs," she said. "And you're Kyle."

"Kyle Cameron." He offered his good hand. "Pleased to meet you, Theresa."

His hand was warm, his grasp firm but not painful. Calluses scraped against her palm. It was a masculine hand, telegraphing strength and confidence. Her heart fluttered again, and she jerked away to fuss with the supplies on the cart. Her skin still tingled from his touch. She laid out the materials she'd need for the tattoo—new packages of needles, fresh ink caps, gauze, sterile wipes, A&D ointment and the tattoo machine, still in its sealed packet from the autoclave.

"I found the one I want." George pointed to a page in the binder.

Theresa walked over and studied the drawing of a snarling monitor lizard. "All right. Have a seat here and we'll get started."

Looking a little apprehensive, George stretched out on the chair.

"You want me to hold your hand?" Kyle asked.

"Only if you want me to break your other arm."

While she prepped George, Kyle settled on a stool across from them, watching as she swabbed the freshly shaved section of George's arm with disinfectant and positioned the tattoo transfer. She switched on the tattoo machine. "You ready, George?"

"Uh, yeah." He blanched. "Sure."

"Don't worry, pard. When you pass out from the pain, I'll help revive you." Kyle winked at Theresa, who steadfastly ignored the way this made her stomach quiver and concentrated on the tattoo.

George made a gurgling sound in his throat when the needles first made contact. She kept a firm grip on his arm and continued working. "Take a deep breath. Relax. Focus on something to distract you."

Predictably, his gaze zeroed in on her chest once more. "Th—that's a real interesting tattoo," he said. "Who did it?"

"My brother."

"He's a tattoo artist, too?" Kyle asked.

"He's the one who taught me."

"I was wondering how a pretty girl like you would get into something like this," George said.

"Right." She switched colors and began outlining the lizard's eyes. "Like I haven't heard that one before."

"I don't know. Sounds like a pretty good job to me," Kyle said. "Good hours. You're pretty much your own boss." He grinned. "And a chance to inflict pain on ugly SOBs like the Lizard here."

As she worked, she could feel Kyle's eyes on her. His stare wasn't the rude ogling of some men, but rather the studious gaze of someone who was trying to figure her out. Ogling she could deal with—she didn't much care for this kind of close scrutiny. "Do you mind?" she said, glaring at him.

"Mind what?"

"You're staring."

"No, I'm watching you."

"Well stop it."

"You interest me."

"Well, cowboys don't interest me, so don't get any ideas."

"Darlin', I've had ideas about you since the minute I laid eyes on you."

The combination of a molasses-sweet drawl and a one-hundred degree gaze was doing a number on her libido. She maintained her grip on the tattoo machine and continued working, the original Ms. Cool. "You and your ideas are going to be very disappointed," she said, ignoring the pinch of regret the words sent through her.

He laughed. "You've done it now."

"Done what?" Why did he look so pleased with himself?

"Saying that is like waving a red flag in front of a bull. There's nothing a man like me enjoys better than a challenge."

She bristled. "That wasn't a challenge."

"Sounded like one to me," George said.

She looked from one man to the other. They were both wearing smart-assed grins. She had half a mind to slap sense into both of them. But that would probably only egg them on. She settled for a return on her Ice Queen routine. "Think what you like," she said. "You'll end up disappointed."

KYLE WATCHED Theresa work. He couldn't remember when he'd met a more intriguing package: sex appeal and sass wrapped up with a heavy dose of smarts.

He was glad he'd let George talk him into coming here this morning, instead of sitting around his borrowed apartment and moping the way he'd done ever since that calf had snapped the bone in his wrist and put an abrupt halt to this season's rodeo competition.

All he had to look forward to now was six weeks of bumming around town or, worse, recuperating at the family ranch, listening to his sister's lectures on responsibility and settling down.

"What do you do when you're not on the rodeo circuit?"

Theresa's question pulled him away from his slide toward a deep blue funk. She was focusing on the lizard taking shape on George's arm, not looking at him, but apparently she'd decided at least to be friendly.

"My family has a ranch out near Wimberley," he said. "But right now I'm just hanging around Austin."

"Oh. So you really are a cowboy."

"I guess you could say that."

"I think I'd be bored out of my skull living way out like that." She shut off the machine and blotted George's fresh tat with gauze. "Guess I'm too much of a city girl."

You and me both, Kyle thought, but he kept quiet. His current restlessness didn't really have anything to do with this woman, though he couldn't help wonder if she wouldn't be a good antidote for what was ailing him. Spending the next six weeks having a good time with a willing woman would be a damn sight more fun than moping around the ranch house.

"What time do you get off work?" he asked.

She looked up, the hard look erased from her face for a moment. For a split second she looked softer. Vulnerable even. Then the mask was back in place. "I told you I wasn't interested."

He let a slow smile form, putting every bit of sex appeal he could muster into the look. "I think I could make things interesting…for both of us."

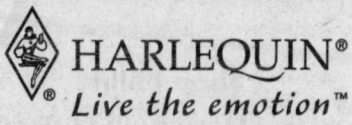

HARLEQUIN®
Temptation.

AMERICAN HEROES

These men are heroes— strong, fearless... And impossible to resist!

Join bestselling authors Lori Foster, Donna Kauffman and Jill Shalvis as they deliver up

MEN OF COURAGE

Harlequin anthology
May 2003

Followed by *American Heroes* miniseries
in Harlequin Temptation

RILEY by Lori Foster
June 2003

SEAN by Donna Kauffman
July 2003

LUKE by Jill Shalvis
August 2003

Don't miss this sexy new miniseries by some of
Temptation's hottest authors!

Available at your favorite retail outlet.

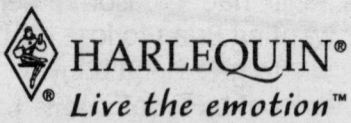

HARLEQUIN®
Live the emotion™

Visit us at www.eHarlequin.com

HTAH

Silhouette®

Desire®

Enjoy the launch of Maureen Child's NEW miniseries

THREE-WAY WAGER

The Reilly triplets bet they could go ninety days without sex. Hmmm.

The Tempting Mrs. Reilly by MAUREEN CHILD

(Silhouette Desire #1652)
Available May 2005

Brian Reilly had just made a bet to not have sex for three months when his stunningly sexy ex-wife blew into town. It wasn't long before Tina had him contemplating giving up his wager and getting her back. But the tempting Mrs. Reilly had a reason of her own for wanting Brian to lose his bet... to give her a baby!

Brenda Jackson

and Silhouette Desire present a hot new romance starring another sexy Westmoreland man!

JARED'S COUNTERFEIT FIANCÉE

(Silhouette Desire #1654)

When debonair attorney Jared Westmoreland needed a date, he immediately thought of the beautiful Dana Rollins. Reluctantly, Dana fulfilled his request, and the two were somehow stuck pretending that they were engaged! With the passion quickly rising between them, would Jared's faux fiancée turn into the real deal?

Available May 2005 at your favorite retail outlet.